Dark Side

John Choi

James Lorimer & Company Ltd., Publishers
Toronto

James Lorimer & Company Ltd., Publishers acknowledges the support of the Ontario Arts Council (OAC), an agency of the Government of Ontario, which in 2015-16 funded 1,676 individual artists and 1,125 organizations in 209 communities across Ontario for a total of $50.5 million. We acknowledge the support of the Canada Council for the Arts, which last year invested $153 million to bring the arts to Canadians throughout the country. This project has been made possible in part by the Government of Canada and with the support of the Ontario Media Development Corporation.

Cover design: Tyler Cleroux
Cover image: Shutterstock

978-1-4594-1155-5
eBook also available 978-1-4594-1153-1

Cataloguing data available from Library and Archives Canada.

Published by:
James Lorimer & Company Ltd.,
Publishers
117 Peter Street, Suite 304
Toronto, ON, Canada
M5V 0M3
www.lorimer.ca

Distributed by:
Lerner Publishing Services
1251 Washington Ave N
Minneapolis, MN, USA
55401
www.lernerbooks.com

Printed and bound in Canada.
Manufactured by Friesens Corporation in Altona, Manitoba, Canada in December 2016.
Job #228990

Chapter 1

My Parents

Within seconds of walking into my parents'
dry cleaning store, I'm being yelled at. They're
not usually mad if I'm here by 6:00. It's only
6:15 now.

"Emerson — where the hell have you
been?!" This is not an exact translation, but
it's the gist of what Mom screams at me in
Mandarin.

"I was at the library, working on a project,"
I answer in English. This is my go-to answer

to this question — sometimes it's actually true. School is all my parents care about, especially now that I'm in grade twelve and applying to university.

"Why haven't you been answering your phone?" She's not loud, but she's furious. I can tell that something is terribly wrong. I'm afraid to ask what. Earlier today I lost my cell. I'd spent hours searching for it. I retraced all my steps a few times and even looked in a bunch of places it couldn't possibly be. No luck.

"I forgot it at school. It's in my locker," I lie. I lie often — I have to. When I don't have my cell tomorrow, that'll be a problem. But right now, I just need to get through this.

"What are you, stupid? How do you forget your phone at school?" I don't think white parents call their kids stupid. My parents call me stupid on a regular basis. "Your father had to go to the hospital." Her face is beet red.

"What happened?" The words come out quietly but I'm worried.

"His arm swelled up — like a watermelon."
She holds her hands out like she is holding a
giant invisible fruit. "I tried to call you when
it was the size of an orange. And I *kept* calling.
Emerson, you are so irresponsible!" This is
usually when she hits me, but she stays seated
on the stool behind the counter. "It just kept
getting bigger and bigger — we had to close the
store so I could go with him."

Everywhere my dad goes, someone has to
tag along and translate for him. I've shared this
duty with my sister since I was five. Lots of
other Chinese parents speak English quite well.
Not my father. Even though he went to college,
he didn't learn English. He's been in Canada
now for over twelve years and can barely put
together a sentence. He knows just enough to
work at the store. His vocabulary only consists
of a few everyday words, but he knows what
martinizing and *cold spot bleaching mean.*
Because my sister's away at college, I should've
been here to go with him. Then my mom

could've kept the store open. I feel like crap. "Is he okay? Is he still at the hospital?"

"No, he's in the back. The doctor said that he's fine, but you know your father." What she means by this is he may look calm, but he's about to erupt, like a pot of boiling oil. He's sitting alone in a pool of shame at his lack of independence. The red on Mom's face means he's been cruel to her. "Go greet him. Go tell him how sorry you are for not coming earlier."

When my father gets mad at me, he yells at Mom. He says that she's a horrible mother. I know he blamed her for not being able to find me, that it was her fault. He thinks of himself as the wise old head of the family, but then he calls us names like some thirteen-year-old girl on Facebook. He can be violent too — more times than I want to remember. My father doesn't handle anger or frustration well. Mom yells a lot, but when Dad yells, he's mean. Mom threatens me too, but when she actually hits me, it doesn't even hurt. It's very different when it's my father. He doesn't hit me often. But the last time he did, I used my arm to shield myself. I couldn't wear a short-sleeved shirt for three weeks. More often, he takes it out on Mom.

"What did the doctor say?" I ask. I'm still worried but I'm also stalling a bit.

"Apparently, your father is allergic to wasp stings. Go talk to him now, before it gets any later." My heart is pounding in my chest. I'm pissed at him for what he's done to Mom, and I'm nervous about facing him too. The last thing I want to do right now is see my father, but I go. The longer he has to wait for me to show up, the crazier he'll get.

The front of the store is small. Once you slip through to the back, it's pretty big, where all the work is done — huge machines, shelves lined with supplies. In one corner, there's a little room with a curtain instead of a wall. Inside it, my dad built a bed out of wood and carpet. My parents take turns napping there in the afternoon, and it's where we eat our meals. My parents open early and close at nine and do all the dry cleaning on-site. It's more work than I think most of our customers imagine.

I take a breath and step in behind the curtain.

"Dad, are you okay?" On top of anger and fear, there's guilt. They wouldn't have fought if I were there to translate. Dad hates to close the store — ever. He'd open 365 days a year if there were any hope of customers. When I was seven, the year they bought the business, I told them we were supposed to close on holidays. My father yelled that we'd starve to death if I ran the store. That Christmas, he was silent coming home from work. He'd had one customer. He opened on New Year's Day and not one person showed up. Since then, he closes the shop exactly ten days each year. The thought of customers showing up to a closed store in the middle of the day would have been painful for him. He must have thought he was going to die.

He's lying on the bed with one arm over his forehead, the other across his stomach. "Do you have any idea how much your mother worried when you didn't answer her calls?" he says in Chinese, without opening his eyes.

He always expects an answer, even to rhetorical questions. "I am sorry," I say, also in Chinese. I've said this a million times before.

He breathes an abrupt sigh and stops himself from saying whatever it was he was going to say. Instead he says, "Go." I stand there, not knowing if I am supposed to try once more to console him. "GO!" He yells this time, his frustration loud and clear. I suppress my own sigh — that would only set him off. I head back to the front.

Despite getting in trouble so often, I still don't know what I'm supposed to do in these situations. If I'd had my phone, I would have rushed to help him. I didn't ignore them on purpose. Still, I feel so bad. I hate this feeling. I hate him for making me feel like this.

Chapter 2

Pushed

I head out to the front of the shop and tell my mom to go back and eat. My parents eat all of their meals at the store, except dinner on Sunday, when we close early. They expect me to come to the store every day because it's important for the family to eat together. Usually, Mom and Dad start dinner together in the corner room, while I mind the counter. Dad hurries through his meal, and then I head back and Mom sits and watches me eat. Mom gets up super early every morning and packs all the food for the day. The little room in the back is equipped with a microwave, toaster oven and a tiny plug-in stove.

Two months ago, the owner of the convenience store next to the dry cleaners was stabbed in the thigh with a screwdriver while being robbed. Just over a year ago, the diner at the end of our strip of stores was robbed at gunpoint. We try to have at least two people at the cleaners if it's possible. I doubt having two of us here would make a difference if we were robbed. But my parents think it's somehow a deterrent. They practically live in this place. I do work alone for a few hours early in the day every Saturday and Sunday so they can have a break. They use the time to go grocery shopping and do house work. I'm worried about what they're going to do when I go away for school next year.

Mom mumbles about not having an appetite and that Dad will refuse to eat. I sigh.

There's no point in arguing.

I open a textbook, hoping I don't have to talk to her.

About ten minutes later, there are a couple of customers in the store. My mom is counting the shirts a man is dropping off for cleaning. One of our regulars is waiting, and she asks me what I'm studying.

"Grade twelve physics." I have an assignment due tomorrow.

She smiles and says, "I didn't do science beyond grade ten." Joyce is in her late twenties and comes in about twice a month. She's one of a handful of Chinese customers that Dad can actually talk to. My parents don't charge Mandarin-speaking people the tax on their cleaning. Plus they'll do small mending jobs, like fixing loose buttons, for free — just because the customer is Chinese.

I'm about to ask her what she studied in university when my dad emerges from the back. He tells me to go and eat.

"I'm not hungry," I answer. I never have an appetite when I'm in trouble. You'd think he'd know this about me.

"I didn't ask you. You need to eat. Go now."

Joyce says hi to Dad. My father gives her a curt greeting. The other customer is done and leaves the store. Mom calls Joyce up to the counter and in the same breath tells me to do what Dad says. I close my textbook. "You two eat, and I'll look after the customer," I say to my mom. I move to take over for her. I'm really not hungry and I'm trying to be helpful.

"Go quickly," she insists.

Before I can respond, Dad grabs my sweatshirt at the shoulder and drags me to the back. He pushes me. I stumble and recover just before slamming into a machine.

"It is bad enough that you are unreliable. Do not disobey me in front of others." He storms off to the front, not giving me a chance to say anything. Mom rushes back and slaps me on the shoulder.

"Your father has had a rough day. Why do you choose to aggravate him?"

"Aggravate him? I was trying to be nice . . ." *And what about the day I've had?*

"You should know better." She's right. I should've known that he'd react that way. Still, I'm seething. And he's worried about what Joyce might think about the way I treated him. What about her seeing how I was treated? I shake my head. This is my family.

* * *

We get home shortly after nine. I head straight for the basement. My bedroom is on the second floor. It's right next to my parents' room and they have no issues barging into mine whenever they feel like it. The main floor of our townhouse has a kitchen, a small dining room and a tiny living room. My parents set up the TV, a big comfortable couch and a card table down here and call it the family room, but they never come down. It's where I spend all my time when I'm at home.

Losing my cell is a big deal. It took me forever to convince my parents to buy it for me. "What does a sixteen-year-old need with a smartphone?" they asked. Never mind that every one of my friends had one. They also wouldn't let me get a part-time job so that I could buy one for myself. "At this age, you should be studying, not wasting time working," they said. Never mind that they expect me to help at the store. It's no surprise my parents didn't want to buy me a phone. Our family car was bought second-hand, and they still wear all the same clothes they brought with them from China twelve years ago. They share a cell between the two of them — it's a freaking flip phone.

Last year they finally gave in and got me my phone. They will lose their minds when they find out I've lost it. *How can I get out of this?* I wrack my brain but I've got nothing.

I've already looked everywhere. I have enough money saved to replace it. There's about $820 in my bank account. It's money I've saved over the years — gifts from aunts and uncles and money I've earned tutoring through a school program. I'd started saving because I always figured one day I'd run away from home. But the thought of dishing out a whack of cash for a phone when mine was perfectly fine hurts my head. Doesn't matter though — the plan's under Dad's name. I couldn't replace it without them finding out.

I notice my backpack out of the corner of my eye. I have a unit test in math tomorrow. There's no way I can study right now. I didn't finish that physics assignment either. I turn on my laptop and put on my headphones.

Chapter 3

Insomnia

Hours later, I roll over and check the clock radio — it's 2:23 a.m. This is ridiculous. I've been trying to get to sleep for over an hour. It's going to be hell getting up tomorrow morning. I'm tired, but this is futile. I wish my mind came with an on/off button. When my thoughts keep cycling through in a nonstop loop, I can't sleep. I ended up not even touching a textbook before finally lying down to try to sleep. I'm too tired to start studying now. I don't know how I can feel so exhausted and wired at the same time.

It feels weird not to have my cell. I keep thinking I feel it vibrate. And then I put my hand where my pocket would be and there's nothing there. I have a laptop, but it's not the same. I have all my apps on the phone. I sigh and try to rub the exhaustion from my eyes. My parents are going to kill me.

I get out of bed and pull on a pair of sweatpants. I grab a hoodie off the floor, slip down the stairs and move quietly out the side door. I'm careful not to make too much noise, even though there is no fear of waking up my parents. They're both heavy sleepers and their room is far enough away. I open the garage and I grab my bike. Now I'm wheeling away, pedalling as fast as I can. I must be going a hundred kilometres an hour. It's kind of cold and dark, but there's something about the feeling of my face cutting through the chill in the air that feels really good. I turn down Spruce Road and head for the lake.

There's a boardwalk that runs along the lakeshore that separates the beach from the road. I drop my bike there and walk toward the water. They call this a beach, and I guess it is, technically. But the sand's not soft or powdery, like the beach at Sandbanks or Sauble. I'd been to real beaches that have sand and clean water with friends and their parents when I was younger. The beach here is equal parts sand and pebbles and rocks — and bottle caps and cigarette butts and other litter. It doesn't smell all that great either. But I like it anyway. I like the sound of the water. It's hard to hear it during the day with all the cars passing by and stuff. Right now it's lapping in a rhythm that makes me forget how tired I feel. I try not to think about my dad, but I can't help it. I throw a rock into the lake. It skips four times.

I imagine taking off to somewhere far away. There's no hope of my dad ever changing. And he's so miserable. A pair of seagulls flies over my head. Don't they ever sleep? I imagine my dad being swarmed by wasps and dying. I feel bad for thinking this. I imagine feeling free if that really happened. I feel bad for thinking this too.

I pick up another rock and throw it as far as I can into the lake. The rock makes a splash as it enters the water. I stare out into the lake and picture myself climbing over the side of a boat. I could canoe way out there — it is really deep near the middle of the lake. If I tied some heavy weights around my ankles, I'd sink to the bottom. I could do this in the middle of the night and the canoe would just float away. Then they wouldn't be able to find me. I think about that for a while.

I worry now about what it would be like for my parents if they had to deal with my dying. I don't like that I worry so much. If I was dead, though, I guess I *couldn't* care. I wonder what happens to people when they die — I mean what *really* happens.

* * *

I drag myself out of bed after about three hours of sleep. Somehow I didn't oversleep. I open my eyes, thinking about my math test. I have this sense that I'm going to fail. I regret not trying harder to study last night, and not doing my homework more consistently the last couple of weeks. I have a spare right after lunch, before the test. I'll study then.

I feel like I'm missing a limb without my cell. I wonder how many texts from my friends might be sitting out there in cyber world. Probably not that many, but still. It's the worst thing ever when you leave someone hanging. How many people are wondering why I blew them off yesterday, ignoring their messages?

I step into the shower. I linger here for a while. I close my eyes and imagine I'm standing under a waterfall and just let it rain on me — showers always feel good after nights when I've hardly slept.

BANG BANG!

Mom is banging on the door. She yells,

"Hurry up! You're going to be late!"

I take off without eating anything for breakfast. I'll have to skip first period. I head to the library to finish the assignment. I can hand it in at lunch. I'll need a reason for missing class, but I'll worry about that later.

I meet my friend Maheen, who has a spare first period. She's got her math book open.

"Hey, how come you weren't answering messages yesterday?" she asks.

"Lost my cell." I sit down beside her.

"Really? That sucks. You're not going to class?"

"Didn't finish my physics project."

Maheen frowns. "Ms. Rosier doesn't accept assignments late without a doctor's note."

"I'm going to try her anyway." I know this might be a problem. But my teachers generally cut me slack.

"Yeah, you'll probably get away with it. Ready for the math test?"

"I'm going to study at lunch."

"You don't even need to study. You're so lucky, Em."

I chuckle. "Yeah right. I'll be lucky not to fail this test."

"Ha! You've never failed a test in your life." Maheen smiles.

"Did you need something, yesterday?"

"I needed some help with this." She nods toward her textbook. "But I got a hold of someone else." Maheen sticks her tongue out at me and smiles again. Then she gets back to solving some problems and I begin to work on my science.

What Maheen said was true, up until last year. I used to get really good marks without trying too hard. In grade nine, most of my marks were in the high 90s. My lowest grade was 88 in gym. But the marks have slipped a bit more in each of the last couple of years. This year is shaping up to be a disaster. Nights like yesterday sure don't help.

Chapter 4

Useless

When I leave English, I decide to blow off student council. We're working on getting the principal to reinstate the prom. Last year, some kids from another school crashed our formal, and they brought drugs and alcohol with them. Prom was cancelled indefinitely after that. I supported council fighting this at first, but now I don't really care. At first, it was the principle behind the issue. It wasn't fair for this year's seniors to suffer for what happened the year before, especially when the offenders weren't even from our school. But now, I'm on the brink of actually failing a test. And it's not like I have anyone to go to the prom with anyway.

Besides, I feel crappy. I wonder if I should head back to the library to sleep for a few minutes before trying to study for math. On top of everything else, I've forgotten my lunch, and my stomach is growling. I go to Pepe's and grab a slice and eat it as I walk back to school. As I step through the opening in the fence that separates our field from the sidewalk, a soccer ball rolls toward me. I kick the ball back to my friend Stuart, who yells at me to come play. They need one more to make the teams even. I'm no jock but I'm not too bad at soccer. Most of these guys play soccer every chance they get, and I join them once in a while. What the hell — why not? I run hard, and I chase the ball down one side near the edge of the field. I kick the ball right at Stuart, who redirects it into the other team's net. Gavin, who's a really good athlete, slaps me on the back and yells, "Sweet!" I play for the next twenty minutes until the bell rings to signify that the period is over. I'm spent, but it was good not to think about crap for a little while.

Lunch is finished, and now I have my spare. I sit in front of my locker. I open my math textbook, but I can't focus. I shut my book and then close my eyes. I'm just too tired. I think about going to the office and signing myself out for the day, maybe complain about feeling sick. But the school requires a doctor's note if you're absent on the day of a test. I have no choice — I'll just have to wing it.

I drag myself to math class. I answer the first question okay. But by the second question, I'm regretting not studying during my double lunch. Why did I play soccer when I could've gotten an hour and a half of studying in? I always do this. I mess up and then I think back to what I could have or should have done. But the truth is, I still don't change my ways or try to fix things. I still leave assignments to the last minute, or I stay up listening to music or texting back and forth with my friends instead of working or sleeping. My stomach churns. I feel like an idiot for not studying, combined with how I usually feel after not sleeping well. I regret not even trying to study. But it wouldn't have helped anyway. I'm too damned tired. My body feels weak. And my head feels cloudy. What I wouldn't do for a nap right now.

* * *

I see Maheen after my last class. "Wanna chill?" I ask.

"Sorry, I've got STEM club. Any luck finding your cell?"

I shake my head. I'm disappointed but not surprised. "See you later."

I see a few other people I could maybe hang out with. But I realize I don't really want to chill with anyone after all.

I walk to the bus stop. I get on and grab a seat halfway back. There are only two other riders, a couple sitting at the rear of the bus.

Without my phone, I feel like a bird that's had his wings clipped. I don't even know what time it is, because my cell was also my watch. Normally, I'd be listening to music or texting with someone all the way home. I don't live that far away, but the traffic is heavy and we're barely crawling along. I wish I'd ridden my bike this morning. I close my eyes for a bit, but I feel restless. I need to come up with something to tell my parents. Maybe that the phone broke and I gave it to someone who could fix it. Then I could tell them that after they took it apart, they found it was unfixable. It's a lame excuse and they would still be mad, but it beats the flat-out truth that I just lost it. When I was eight, I lost my backpack. Actually, it was stolen. I had put it down while I played soccer with my buddies in the park after school. When I was ready to go home, it was gone. Losing my backpack prompted my parents to tell me how miserable their lives have been, how I should be grateful for all their sacrifices and that I'd brought shame to the family.

I know that I will hear this all over again tonight, and I will tune most of it out. Most of it, but not all of it. I shake my head. I can tell myself they're screwed up. They are. But if they're the ones who are messed up, why do I feel this guilt?

I grab the newspaper left on the seat next to me. The headline is about a mass murder that had happened yesterday morning in the States. Two dozen kids were killed in a school. On the next page, there's a story about how elderly people are being scammed out of their retirement savings. I skim through the article. I get upset reading stuff like this. Innocent people suffering at the hands of bad people. Then I go from feeling mad to feeling depressed. I turn the page. There's another article about the guy who committed the mass murder from the first page. It tells how he'd been bullied and abused as a kid. I toss the paper aside. I can't read this stuff.

The guy and girl in the back of the bus are arguing now. Once I notice, I can't help but hear what they're saying.

"I can't go with you." The girl's wearing a tight-fitting aqua-coloured jacket.

"Why not? It's just one night — and it's all paid for. Your crazy mother's not even going to notice you're not at home." He's much taller than she is.

"Don't call her that." She looks away.

"You know it's true. Are you worried about getting pregnant like her? You don't have to worry — I'm not as stupid as your lazy-ass father." He shakes his head.

"I should never have told you anything." Her hair is long and straight. The colour is something between brown and red.

"You're lucky a guy like me even gives a shit about you. I care about you, Max. Don't you get that?" He's got really short blond hair. She tries to get up and he grabs her wrist. He pulls her back into her seat. She looks away. Her eyes are wet and puffy. I didn't hear the beginning of their argument, but she doesn't deserve this. Maybe I should say something. "Look at me when I talk to you!" His teeth are clenched. "It's always all about you!" He's gripping the upper part of her arm and he shakes her.

"Damn it, Nico — it hurts when you do that!"

Why does stuff like this happen? I can feel myself getting hot around my neck. I imagine myself getting up and going back there. I could just say to him, "Hey buddy, why don't you cool down a bit?" Or ask the girl if she's okay. I could do that.

But I don't. I'm not sure why I can't. He's getting louder.

"I'm barely touching you!" he snaps.

I'm sitting on a seat that's facing sideways, so I can see them without turning my head in their direction. I lean forward in my seat. Okay, I'm going to just say something. Still, I don't move. Why doesn't the driver do anything? Isn't it part of his job to do something? It's my stop. I look toward the back and get up. Now or never. The guy glares at me. I just get off the bus.

I suck.

Chapter 5

Charged

I lied to my parents about having to do group work. I come straight home without stopping at the store today. When my parents arrive after closing, they're both in a crappy mood. There is no "hi honey, how was your day at school?" the way I imagine white parents would ask.

"There is $608 worth of charges on your cell phone account," my mom informs me.

I feel like I've been hit by truck. It didn't

occur to me that whoever found my phone could be running up charges.

"When you didn't respond to our calls again today, we knew you must have lost your phone, so I called the phone company to suspend your plan," explains my mom.

So much for the lie I was going to tell.

"Emerson, you didn't rack up all these charges, did you?" I shake my head, still in shock. *$608*. "Whoever has your phone must have used it to call long distance — somewhere quite far away," my mother says.

I sink into a chair. I mumble, "It's probably data. There's only 200 megs on the plan. You burn that much just by turning the phone on."

The lecture begins.

I can feel my stomach travel up in my chest. The volume of their voices hasn't started to rise yet — they're just warming up. What gets me is that they repeat the same things over and over again. I think I'm tuning them out, but somehow I hear every single word. *Stupid — sacrifices*

— foolishness — irresponsible — when they were young — and so on — and so on.

There's a knock on the front door. We never get unexpected visitors. I'm grateful for the distraction, even though it's only likely to last for a minute or two. It can only be someone looking for donations or someone wanting to talk about buying a plan for natural gas or something like that. I get up to answer the door, because it's also my job to chase these people away. My parents only donate money to charity once a year — $20, around Chinese New Year, to orphans in mainland China.

When I get up, though, I see through the window that a police car is parked in the driveway. There is no sound from the sirens, but the lights are flashing. I open the door to two uniformed officers. The tall one on the left says, "We're looking for Emerson Yeung."

I tell the cops that I'm Emerson, and my mom comes and stands behind me. She asks me in Chinese why they're here.

The shorter of the two officers is a white woman with her hair tucked neatly under her cap. She introduces herself as Constable Fisher, and her partner as Constable Williams. She asks if they can come in. I open the door fully and lead them to the kitchen. They sit themselves down at the table. Neither of them take off their shoes. My parents don't ask them to, either. I guess the police have special status with my parents. I've never seen them let someone in the house with their shoes on. I'm thinking the cops are probably not allowed to take their shoes off, but my parents wouldn't know that. The police officers do remove their caps.

"We're here because of the recent posts on your Facebook page, Emerson," says Constable Williams. He's tall, black and looks like he's in his late 20s. His uniform shirt is short-sleeved and his biceps are huge.

Was it something someone else had posted to my wall? Was one of my friends in trouble and they were here to get me to confirm something? I hate being put on the spot. I like to prepare responses ahead of time.

"I haven't been on Facebook in a couple days. I lost my phone yesterday, so I haven't even seen any alerts in over twenty-four hours," I say.

"You lost your phone yesterday?" Constable Fisher asks.

"But you can still access Facebook from any computer," Constable Williams adds.

"Sure, I know that, but I only ever go on from my phone."

"What is this about? Did my son do something wrong?" my mother interjects with a calm and even tone. I know she is getting anxious about what the problem might be. She's also worrying about how my dad is getting angrier in the corner of the room, frustrated at not being able to join the conversation.

"Was your phone lost or stolen?" Constable Fisher asks.

"I don't know. I guess it could have been

stolen," I reply.

"Did you report it?"

"No, I thought I'd just lost it. I was kind of hoping I'd find it today."

"What is this about?" my mother asks again, her Chinese accent even stronger than usual.

Constable Fisher pulls out some sheets of paper from a file folder. She spins the first one so it's right-side up from where I'm sitting. It's a screenshot of a photo. It shows a gun pointed at Mr. Selvadurai's face. He's my vice principal. Under the picture is the caption, "quit or die u Muslim terrorist."

The next image Constable Fisher shows me is of another gun pointed at a photograph of Ms. McAdam, one of teachers at my school. It's been taken from last year's yearbook. This one has the caption, "Go to hell with the sand monkeys!" Ms. McAdam spends a lot of time helping students after school, especially students who are new to Canada. In the last couple of years, we've had lots of kids start at MCI who have literally just arrived in the country.

Both posts appear to have been put up by me.

"Are you aware, Emerson, that these constitute actual threats?" Constable Williams asks.

I feel my heart drop into my stomach. "I didn't do this." My voice is quieter than I intended. I feel so stupid. I leave myself logged into my account all the time. Anyone who had a hold of my phone could post anything and people would think it was me.

"This is your Facebook account," Constable Williams says. It's not a question. It's obvious that it's my account. My face is very clearly in the profile-picture spot. "Have you been having any troubles at school?"

"No." I shake my head.

"You'll be much better off telling us the truth, Emerson, and not hiding anything," Constable Fisher says.

I'm not sure what I'm supposed to say. I've only ever been to Mr. Selvadurai's office once

— for skipping class. He gave me a warning and let me go. If anything, I was grateful to him for not telling my parents.

"You do know both of these folks?" Constable Williams asks, pointing to the two pages.

"Mr. S is my VP and Ms. McAdam teaches English."

"And how are you doing in English this year?"

I hesitate for a second. "Okay." There's a big assignment due next week that I haven't started yet.

"Are you having any issues with your teacher?"

I shake my head.

"What about the other students in your school?"

"I get along fine with everybody." This was true.

"Do you have any issues with Middle Eastern kids?"

"No." I've heard some other students complain that the newcomers were getting a lot of attention from the teachers, and that they were getting special treatment. It's never bothered me, though. "I don't have a problem with anyone." Except maybe my parents, but that's another story.

Mom asks me in Chinese, "What is going on?"

I thought it was pretty obvious. I explain as briefly as I can.

Constable Fisher turns to my mom and asks her, "Are you aware of any trouble Emerson is having at school?"

"No." Mom is emphatic. "He is a very good student."

Dad says to me in Chinese, "What do they want?" I try to explain again but he cuts me off. "What idiotic thing have you done that makes the police come here?"

"I didn't do anything," I try to tell him.

Mom turns to Dad and says, "Be still." This means, *please, that is not helpful right now.*

He replies, "Tell them that this is ridiculous."

Constable Williams turns to Dad and asks, "Has Emerson ever engaged in violent behaviour?"

Dad looks blankly at him and turns to me. Mom quickly answers, "No. Never."

"And what about Emerson's friends? Do his associations concern you at all?"

I start with a translation. She talks over me, looking right into the officer's eyes. "Emerson has only good friends. He is a good boy." The last time Mom or Dad met any of my friends was back in middle school. I guess those are the ones she's referring to. I haven't seen them in years.

Constable Williams asks, "Do you mind if we look around the house?"

I feel insulted by this. I ask, "Don't you need a search warrant for that?"

"Not if your parents give us permission."

I turn to Mom and tell her in Chinese that she doesn't have to let them. She smacks me on the shoulder, and Dad tells me to be still.

They look around our entire house, spending extra time in my room going through all my drawers and my backpack. They ask me if they could take my laptop with them to have a forensics specialist examine it. Before I can answer, Mom tells them, "Yes, if it will help."

"But I need that for school. When will I get it back?"

"Can't promise. Likely in a week? As long as it doesn't become evidence," Constable Fisher answers. I'm biting my lip now. I want to argue with them but it would only set my parents off.

I guess the police could see I was pissed. "It's to your benefit to cooperate, Emerson. This is a very serious matter. These threats are a criminal offense." Constable Williams stares into my eyes.

As they finally leave, I feel the knot in my stomach get tighter. Having the police accuse me of a crime was bad. But the truth is I'm more afraid of my father.

Chapter 6

Blame

The second I close the door, the barrage starts.

It begins exactly as I expect it to.

"How can you be so irresponsible?!" Dad yells. He bangs his fist on the table. "Why are you trying to ruin our lives?!"

Right, I got falsely accused of a crime because I want to ruin your life.

Then comes all the usual stuff about everything they've done for me. He tries to wring out every tiny bit of guilt I could possibly have. I swear, if he had this much passion for anything else, he'd win all kinds of awards.

"Your mother is sick all the time! This is because you cause her so much worry!" It's true that both my parents complain all the time about not feeling well. I think it's because they're constantly exposed to dangerous dry-cleaning chemicals, but try telling them that.

The word *sacrifices* is hurled at me like rock. I stare at a chipped tile on the floor. I've heard all of this before. So many times. I'm mad at myself for not being able to just tune this out. *I didn't ask for anything.*

"We should never have left China! If this police thing doesn't resolve itself, you are going back!"

I imagine myself on some farm with only my relatives to talk to — no friends, no Internet. If he knew about my math test, my dad would probably pack my bags tonight. I feel tears forming in my eyes. I clench my fists and do everything I can to hold the tears there, to not let them drop.

I bite my lip. At school, teachers always tell you to walk away from conflict. But the teachers at school don't know my parents. Mom mumbles under her breath, "Why is this child like this? Where did he pick this stuff up?" I can hear every word, but it makes no sense to me.

"Well?" my dad asks.

But there was no question. I'm somehow supposed to read his mind. Usually, if I've done something wrong, I'd apologize at this point in the routine. But I didn't do anything this time. I look up at him. I know that this is not a good idea, because the look on my face is a combination of confusion, disgust and contempt.

Dad is getting madder, but so am I. His face is growing redder, and I feel mine burning hot. He's waiting me out. My mom says in the quietest voice, "Emerson, apologize and go study."

Dad tells Mom to be still. In this case, he means *don't interfere*, or maybe, *don't try to help him*. I'm still staring at him. *Why is he like this?* His head is actually quivering now. He slaps me. On the face, hard.

Then he leaves the room.

Mom gets up and slaps me on the shoulder. "Why? Why do you do this?"

Do what? My eyes are full of tears now because I'm so angry. I give Mom a look of disbelief and go downstairs. I don't feel like doing anything. I lie down on the couch. I feel like maybe I should talk to someone, but there is no one to talk to. I'm exhausted.

Somehow I fall asleep.

I start to have one of those dreams that feels really real. I'm in a long hallway in some kind of hospital. I think I smell bleach. I'm standing outside a door with a small window. I look in and see the girl from the bus, the one wearing the aqua jacket. She's lying on the bed in the room, all alone. She's bruised — her entire face is swollen and purple. Her arm is in a cast, hanging from a metal bar. I zoom into her face and I see pus oozing out of the cuts and scrapes. She looks straight into my eyes. She wants to ask me something. "Why didn't you help me when you saw me getting yelled at on the bus?" I want to throw up. I go to the next room.

I see my father — he stands next to the bed. Mom lies there with her eyes closed. Dad pulls the sheet over her, covering her entire head. Then he turns and sees me. He comes out of the room. He slaps me in the face. I am frozen. He grabs my wrist. His bloodshot eyes are almost entirely red. "We are going back to China," he says to me in Chinese. I pull free and run down the hall as fast as I can. But in this dream, I can't run. It's like I'm running through quicksand. All of a sudden, I jerk forward and crash through another door. I'm on a staircase and I fall to over. My friends from school are all running away from me — some

up the stairs, some down. Maheen's there —
she glances over her shoulder and gives me a
look, like she's disgusted with me. Then the
police burst through the door and jump me. I
jolt awake, breathing hard.

I get up and turn on my ancient desktop
— and open Facebook. I've been logged off
— weird. I leave myself on all the time. I try
to get back in. A pop-up message says that my
account has been suspended. *Great.*

I wonder if whoever took my phone has
sent any messages to my friends, or posted stuff
on their walls pretending to be me. No one said
anything at school today. No one mentioned
the threats. I hadn't been called to the office.
All of this must have happened while I was at
school or after. I guess I should be happy they
shut my account down — before any more
damage was done. I try to open the messenger
app but it's been shut down too. Without my
phone, I'm completely cut off from my friends.
I am pissed. I hate knowing that someone's

been messing with my identity — messing with me. This is the worst.

I try to get some homework done, but I can't focus. School is getting harder, so I really should be doing my homework and studying. But it's so hard to concentrate. I give up after a while. I put on my headphones and listen to music.

I try a couple of times to go back to my schoolwork again, but I just can't get going. That English assignment is due next week and I haven't even decided on a topic yet. I keep telling myself to catch up with my math homework too. Even though we had the test today, the stuff is still going to show up on the exam.

Eventually, I give up altogether. I go upstairs to my room. I'm still really tired. My nap was short and won't come close to making up for all the sleep I haven't had the last couple of nights. I lie down and close my eyes. I just want to turn my thoughts off and sleep. I feel light-headed. My stomach hurts. My head hurts now too. I am so freaking tired, so *why can't I sleep*? This is twisted. *God. Please.*

Problems with my parents go back as far as I can remember, from when I was little. These problems with my sleep have been happening for over a year now. I feel stupid for losing my phone. What would have happened if I had just told my parents when I lost it? Maybe they would have shut it down right away and none of this would have happened. Life would be easier if I could just trust my parents, if I didn't have to worry about how crazy they get every time I mess up. I wish that for once, my parents would do something to help me. Or at least help me to not feel so bad. These thoughts roll through my head like a movie, over and over again.

Chapter 7

Hang

I've had thoughts about killing myself since I was eight. I've imagined my parents dying too, like that would somehow solve all my problems. But then I think about all the other reasons for feeling depressed. At that point, I'd return to the suicidal thinking.

I'd start to wonder what the point to everything was. Why should I try so hard? Why put up with the crap? When people feel this bad, other people look at them and think *he's drowning in self-pity.* They say things like "don't you know there are people way worse off than you?" They're talking about people dying in famines or being killed randomly by dictators or working in sweatshops or abused in church basements. Of course these people are worse off. I know that. But what I can't understand is how the hell that's supposed to make me feel better. When I hear that stuff — about other people suffering — I feel even worse. I feel like I'm swimming against the current, and drowning is the only way to escape. Eventually, the feeling would pass, and I wouldn't think about it for a while.

But lately, it feels different. It's like there are clouds following me around, casting darkness wherever I go. The fights with my parents are happening pretty much nonstop now. They say that everything they do is for my sake. But they're so angry or upset or tired or sick all the time. Now there's this mess with the police and my cell phone. And I'm having trouble with school. It's just going to get worse. I can't live like this.

I wonder what things might be like if I weren't around. My parents wouldn't have to work so hard. They have savings to pay for my university tuition that they could use for early retirement instead. They spend so much time and energy worrying about me. They wouldn't have to anymore if I were dead. Retire early and not worry so much. They'd be healthier. My sister might miss me, but she's already in college and she's got a lot going on in her life. She'll be fine. Wouldn't everyone be better off without me around?

There is a feeling of relief in this way of thinking. It's illogical to keep putting myself through miserable day after miserable day. But how would I do it?

* * *

An hour later, I still can't sleep. I tiptoe to the

basement computer and do a Google search. When I have the words "how to" in the field, Google offers a bunch of suggestions like "how to tie a tie." When I add the word "commit," it suggests "how to commit to a goal." When I start to type "suicide," all the suggestions disappear. *That's funny, Google.* Are they worried that by completing the word "suicide," they might be planting the idea in someone's head? Is this a liability thing? What BS. Anybody researching killing themselves has thought about it long before Google puts the thought in their heads. Who's going to be influenced to do something so extreme just because Google suggests it? I shake my head.

Once I get the whole word in, the suggestions come again. Top on the list is "how to commit suicide painlessly." This sounds good. I click.

The first website listed is called "Lost All Hope." Sounds about right. I click again and I get a pop-up. It asks me to confirm that I'm over eighteen years of age. What is this? Protect the kids from dangerous information? Great security measure — ha! I shake my head and pretend to be eighteen. The site opens.

There is a ton of information here about suicide. Apparently, for every successful suicide, there are twenty-five unsuccessful attempts. I have no idea who is writing this stuff or if any of it is legit. There are a bunch of pages on the site that try to talk you out of killing yourself. But then it also ranks the effectiveness of the various methods. The top five require a gun, cyanide or explosives. I don't have access to any of these things. Number six is getting hit by a train, and number seven is hanging. Both of these are listed as about 90 per cent lethal. I'm not quite sure what that means. I guess that nine out of ten people who get hit by a train or hang themselves die? I think about trains in the area. There are tracks close by. I don't like the idea of the train driver having to deal with having killed someone though. I Google "hanging."

I get 350 million results in less than one second. Wikipedia has two separate entries. There are instructions as to how to do it right and warnings about how to screw it up. I sit up in my chair. It's weird how calm I feel. I read some more. It's after three o'clock in the morning. I go back up to my room and try again for some sleep. In my head, I see a sheet of plain white paper and a gallows that someone has drawn for a game of hangman. I see my face where the head would be drawn. I can't get this image to leave me. Now I'm feeling kind of sad. But hanging is a good idea. If I left home, how would I support myself? I'd live with constant guilt about my parents and be depressed about all the other stuff that happens in the world. I need to figure out when. I suppose the sooner the better. I can't do it right this minute though. I'm too tired. Maybe tomorrow. I nod to myself. *Maybe tomorrow.*

Chapter 8

Bad

The next morning, I have the worst time getting up. I think I got about three hours of sleep. I rush to get ready for school. I splash water on my face — it's way too late to shower. I need today to make sure I've had a chance to think about loose ends. There might be things I need to do before I go. If I miss school, they'll call home and it'll just start a new snowball of trouble that I don't want any part of.

I run into the school just as the bell is ringing. My principal, Mr. Leeder, is standing by my locker. He asks me to join him in his office and starts walking. I follow and he lets me know that he's called my mother and has asked her to join us as well. He says that she'll be here shortly. My stomach sinks.

I wait on the hard wooden bench in the student office for thirty minutes. When my mother arrives, she does not look happy. She doesn't even bother to say hi. "Why are you waiting here — couldn't they let you stay in class at least until I got here?" She's worried that I missed thirty minutes of gym? Mr. Leeder must have seen my mother drive up because he comes out to ask us into his office.

As soon as we sit, he starts. "Mrs. Yeung, the threats from Emerson's Facebook account are very serious and have caused a high level of concern. The board has very strict rules regarding online social-media conduct and even stricter rules about violence." His entire neck is red and parts of his face are blotchy. He's the principal of a school with over a thousand students, and he's talking to a little Chinese woman and one of the least troublesome kids at our school.

Why is he so nervous?

"Mr. Leeder, we spoke to the police. It's a mistake. I didn't post those threats. Someone stole my phone," I say.

My mother chips in. "Mr. Leeder, my son is a good boy." I hate that phrase — *a good boy* — and I cringe. This is how she talks.

A yawn escapes my mouth — I can't help it. Mom smacks me on the shoulder. She thinks it's disrespectful. It's a function of biology though. I didn't do it on purpose.

Mr. Leeder says, "I'm aware that the police are involved. This is very serious, Emerson. The threats came from your account."

"After my phone was stolen, sir." It was one thing for the police to accuse me. Mr. Leeder *knows* me.

"I've spoken to all your teachers. Each one of them was surprised. But a couple of them noted that you seem disconnected from your friends lately. In any case, you are suspended from your classes indefinitely."

"Suspended?! But, sir, I didn't post those pictures! Someone else did it using my phone!" I sound desperate. I've never been suspended before.

My mother asks me in Chinese what this means.

I explain. She grimaces like someone's smacked her in the face. "But Emerson did not commit a crime," my mother pleads.

"I'm sorry, Mrs. Yeung. I don't have a choice in the matter. Even if the situation is resolved with the police, Emerson will have to apply to the board to have the suspension withdrawn."

I know Mom is wishing that her English were better. I don't think it would have helped though. We leave the school, both of us feeling powerless. I can't believe this is happening to me.

We drive to the dry cleaners. When my father sees me with my mother, his face turns red immediately. I swear I can almost see smoke starting to come out of his ears. I head straight to the back. There is a pile of clothing that needs sorting. I'm hoping that if I get to work right away, maybe they might leave me alone. Even as I think this, I know there is no way. After about a minute, Dad comes to the back, proving me right. "What happened at school?" he demands.

I manage to hold back a sigh before answering. "Didn't Mom tell you? I was suspended. The school has rules about what kids write on social media."

"They think you made those threats? Why didn't you tell them that you didn't do it?" Dad has a knack for asking stupid questions. I grit my teeth and take a breath. Today, my patience is thin. I'm tired from not getting any sleep.

Honestly, I'm sick of *everyone* being so freaking stupid. The principal knows me well enough to know that I didn't do it. My parents should understand that this is just how the school system works. Didn't they have any school rules like this in China?

"Even if they believe me, there has to be proof that I didn't do it. When the police clear this up, I'll be allowed to go back," I try to explain.

"It's been fifteen hours since the police came. Why haven't they done anything yet?" He asks the question as if I have an answer. I'm not sure if this is a problem for other immigrant kids or just with my father. Most of my friends are white, brown and black. Sometimes I wish I had some Chinese friends, maybe other kids with my problems. My Canadian friends never seem to go through this crap.

My father starts to sort clothes, so I get back to it too. I took his question to be rhetorical, but my silence pisses him off. "Why haven't the police done anything? Are you sure you weren't the one who made those threats?" he asks.

I'm in shock. "I told you I didn't do it!"

"It is your responsibility. If you hadn't lost your phone, none of this would have happened. We should never have bought you a phone." He doesn't know when to give it a rest.

Forget you — how are you going to feel when I'm dead? I bite my tongue. If I say something more, he'll lose it.

He looks at me, waiting for a response. I can't remember now if he's even asked me a question. What does he want me to say?

"Well?" he says. I'm pretty sure he didn't ask me a question.

"What?" I ask back.

He looks at me in disbelief. He calls me stupid. I don't know why I'm so sensitive to this. He's called me stupid my whole life. You'd think I'd be used to it by now, but no. I feel my eyes welling up, I'm so mad. "Why don't you learn to speak English?" I say. This doesn't even make any sense in this context, but I lash out with something to hurt him. This pushes him over the edge. He raises his hand — but I step back before he can hit me.

"You come here." It's as if to say *How dare you avoid being hit?* I'm about to lose it. I shake my head. I'm nearly ready to hit *him*.

"You are still a child. You expect to be treated like an adult — yet you only do stupid things. A father shouldn't have to tolerate this." He doesn't hesitate this time and smacks me across the face, making a loud slap, like a hockey stick whacking a puck. My cheek stings and I can feel the blood rush to my face.

I take a slow and deep but quivering breath. I look at my father. He seems surprised — maybe he didn't mean to hit me so hard. I'm crying now. I'd managed to hide my tears from him for years, but now I feel like I've been pushed off the ledge.

"I am trying my best. The only way for you to be *relieved* from *tolerating this* is for me not to be here," I say with the quiver in my breathing even more pronounced.

I turn and storm out of the back, tears streaming down my face — I don't even bother wiping them away. I don't care anymore. Dad yells something after me, but I don't hear the words.

"Emerson!" Mom calls me. I ignore her too. I just look straight ahead and keep walking — out of the store, down the street. I expect her to chase me, but she doesn't. *Whatever.* I'm so done with this. With everything. How can I respect my father? How can I listen to that? I walk the twelve blocks home, knowing I will never come back to the store again.

Chapter 9

Why Not?

I go into the garage and find some rope. It's not very thick. This will break for sure. I look around the basement. Nothing I can use. The last place I look is the cold storage room. I see that there are a few boxes in the corner. I take a peek at the contents and find paintings and drawings. I had forgotten about my dad's one attempt to try to make his life better here in Canada. He had a dream of becoming an artist. He'd never had any formal training, but he was really talented. He used to draw nature scenes and liked to draw tigers in particular. It was really impressive.

Dad had applied to a community college here in Toronto and to an art academy in the US. I remember my sister filled out the applications. My dad worked really hard putting together a portfolio of artwork. Then one day, a couple of months later, he threw all of his drawings out. We asked what had happened but he refused to talk about it. I figured he got rejected. We told him he was really good and that he could apply again. But every time Alice or I said something, he just got madder and yelled louder. Sometime later, Mom told me that he found out that he'd been accepted to both schools, but he had to pass an English exam. When he failed every practice test he tried, he gave up. That was years ago.

Painting was the only thing my dad enjoyed. I've often thought if he'd only stuck with it, maybe he wouldn't be so mad all the time. In the box are some drawings of tigers and giraffes. There is a portrait of me and another one of my sister. Even now, I'm looking at them and thinking that they're really good. I feel sad. I notice a white plastic bag next to the box. More paintings? I peek inside. It's a diorama I made when I was in grade three. I remember it clearly because I worked so hard, determined to make my dad proud. But the day I finished it was also the day I got my report card. The teacher made a comment to the effect that I should be trying harder. My dad was just angry that night and didn't really look at my artwork. I remember crying and throwing out the diorama. How is it that it's here in the basement? This is Dad's stuff. Did he salvage this from the garbage? And keep it all this time? Why? There is so much I will never understand.

I don't have time for this now. I get on my bike and ride over to Home Hardware.

I'm surprised to see so many types of rope. They're on huge spools suspended from high shelves. A man asks for his rope to be cut five metres. I try to remember the ideal length for a quick hanging. Five metres sounds good, should be more than enough. I ask the sales guy to cut me a piece. My voice comes out trembling a little. I hope really hard that he doesn't notice. He doesn't look at me weird or anything. He hands me the rope after labelling it for the cashier. My hand is trembling now too, and my heart is beating hard enough that it nearly chokes me. I walk up and down the aisles breathing deeply and slowly. I don't want to make the cashier suspicious. I wonder if the people who sell the guns or ropes or bleach or drugs that their customers use to kill themselves ever get suspicious or find out after. I pay using my debit card. The cashier hands me the receipt and tells me to have a good day. I shove the rope into my backpack and hurry out of the store. I head for home. I'll go to the park tonight after dark.

Once I'm home, I go online and back to the websites on suicide. I come across a forum called WHY NOT? People post short stories about why their lives suck. Each sentence ends with *SWN?* which I soon figure out stands for *so, why not?*

Others post responses trying to talk people out of killing themselves. "Think about the people you're leaving behind — how hard will it be for them . . . ?" "You're a special person — it would be such a waste . . ." "There's help out there . . ." The suicidal people are more interesting. One guy is being bullied at school. Twice, he's been stripped completely naked and pushed out into the hallway, then locked out of the change room. I can see that happening once, but how does that happen a second time to the same person? Another one's failed out of college, he has over $20,000 in debt and he says he has no friends.

A brand-new one appears. The icon indicates she's a girl. Her ID is Frmda6. *From the 6.* It kills me that she's creating an ID for a suicide forum and she makes the effort to come up with something cool like that. I shake my head. Still, according to her ID, she must be from Toronto, so of course I'm curious.

Why not? Really why not??

Posted by Frmda6 just now

I live with my crazy strung out mom SWN?
My little sister is messed up too. She's doing
drugs and won't listen to me SWN? My dad
is hardly around anymore and when he does
come by, he hurts my mom SWN? I don't
remember the last day when I didn't cry SWN?
Why does love have to HURT so much??

I wonder if she's really thinking about killing herself, or if she's just looking for sympathy. I wonder if she's just sitting in front of her computer waiting for responses to appear. One does — that was fast! Beentheredonethat312 suggests that she should try to be more understanding of her family

72

members and that she needs to be strong for them. I imagine that the responder might tell me the same thing. I click the icon to post a response. I have to make an ID first. It's a simple form — confirm age (must be over fourteen, I wonder why fourteen?), gender, email address and choose an ID. I go with Frmda62. I can be clever too. I write: "What do you mean why does love have to hurt?"

I stare at the screen for a few seconds. I'm just about to move on to another page, when there's a response to my response:

I'm with someone but we fight a lot.

A couple of seconds and uhvf8th adds a post beneath her answer:

Just leave him. No guy is worth it. You should leave your family too. You can make it on your own. Believe in yourself!

Wow! These people are fast. I notice an IM function on the page. I click and select Frmda6.

Me: r u finding these answers helpful at all?

Frmda6: not really. r u really from TO?

Me: yeah. u?

Frmda6: yeah. u don't seem like the other people on the site. how come ur here?

Me: just curious I guess . . . r u ok?

Frmda6: . . .

Me: stupid question — sry

Frmda6: dun b sry. i'm ok — someone else just posted that my sister needs me more than ever. i kno they r rt

Me: its hard when ur always having to b strong for others . . . even if they r ur family

Frmda6: right??

Me: y does everyone alwys feel like they hv to talk u out of killing urself?

Frmda6: . . . i'm not sure I want to do it. guess that's y I posted to the site.

Me: rt. That's good, I mean, it's a way of reaching out for help?

Frmda6: I guess. There's no one I can talk to without feeling judged.

Me: I kno what u mean.

We go on like this for like an hour. Turns out her mother has actual mental health problems. She sees a psychiatrist and takes medication. But still she's not well.

> Frmda6: I think my lil sis is stressed about my
> mom. She's started hanging with a bad crowd. I'm
> sure she gets lit a cpl of times a wk.

> Me: have u tried talking to her?

> Frmda6: we always end up fighting.

She tells me about her abusive dad, who doesn't seem to care about her or her sister much. And her boyfriend is the jealous type. He sounds abusive too.

I end up telling her about my parents. I tell her why I was on the site in the first place, that I'd had similar thoughts about killing myself too. I never thought I'd talk to anyone about this stuff but I guess that's what this site is for. We message for a while, and I tell her about losing my phone, then getting framed and questioned by the police.

Eventually, she says:

gotta go. thks for listening . . . n sharing.

Me: np. u too

Frmda6: . . . no judging

Me: no judging . . .

I feel calm. It's been a while since I've felt calm.

Chapter 10

Really?

I spring up all of a sudden. I'm sitting on the
basement couch. It's pitch black down here.
I must have fallen asleep. I can't believe it's
already after one in the morning. I spent the
past eleven hours watching TV, playing games
on the desktop and sleeping. Eleven of my final
hours doing nothing. Not exactly going out
with a bang, but whatever.

I watch a YouTube video and make sure to
set up my noose properly. I find out that two

metres is enough of a drop for my neck to snap. I cut the rope there. If it's too long, the head can snap right off the body. My goal isn't to make the headlines. The *Toronto Sun* would put me on the front page if I decapitated myself. I sneak out of the house and jump on my bike.

I ride toward Cherry Park. There is hardly anyone on the streets. I pass a bus that's empty except for the driver. In the park, there is no one. I head for the bridge. As it comes into view, I see that there's someone there. It has to be nearly two in the morning. Who the hell is in the park at two in the morning? I can see that it's a girl. What is she doing? She's tying a rope to the railing of the bridge. I stop dead in my tracks. Sure, people try to kill themselves every day. But two people, same method, the same bridge, on the same night? What stupidly rotten luck.

What should I do? Give this person her space . . . and just wait my turn? Should I offer to help? With the research I've done, I feel like a bit of an expert. If she's got the wrong length of rope, or it's too weak, or the wrong knot, she's going to either fail her attempt or slowly choke to death. What would I even say? *Excuse me, I couldn't help but notice you were about to commit suicide and I thought I could help?* With my luck, I'd help her, and the police would get here before I do me. I'd end up in jail for assisting in someone else's suicide. While I'm going through this in my head, she notices me.

She's startled. Her face is whiter than the moon that's hanging low in the sky just behind her. I have half a thought to get back on my bike and ride away. But I'm frozen to the spot. I know this person. I'm not sure from where. She doesn't move or say a word. This is awkward. I should say something. I manage to get out the word hi.

That's when I recognize her. The bus. She's the girl from the bus who I saw getting yelled at by her boyfriend. The same hair — the colour I can't figure out, same aqua windbreaker. The girl from my dream. She's here in Cherry Park and she's holding a rope that's tied to the rail of a bridge. I feel my brain pounding against my skull.

My instinct is to try to get her to change her mind. She's crying out for help — right? It's something programmed in my mind by the mental health talks at school, or maybe watching too many movies. I try to think of something to say but the words are stuck in my throat. It's because I feel like a hypocrite. I am a hypocrite. This is uncharted territory. What can I possibly say?

I take a couple of steps toward the bridge. "Um, I don't suppose that you're building a swing with that rope?" I sigh inside my head. I am so lame.

"Can you just go, please? This isn't what it looks like. I'm fine," she finally says.

Crap. She wants me to go away. What did I think she was going to say? *Thanks for showing up?*

I say the next thing that pops into my head. "It's kinda late. Not good to be out alone at this hour. If you want, I could just hang with you for a bit." I wince at my choice of words — how stupid! She doesn't flinch though. I hope she doesn't think I'm an idiot.

"I can't sleep. I don't feel like going home," I say. I'm grateful I managed to say something normal. There's no response, she's just staring downward. I climb the steps onto the bridge. The sky's clear now but everything's still wet from the rain earlier tonight.

"So, what's your excuse for being out in the park alone in the middle of the night?" I keep going. "There are a lot of weirdos out here." Still no smile. At least she's not freaking out, as I half-expected her to. I know the worry makes no sense. I'm essentially in her position — or would have been if she weren't here. She's still not saying anything. I search my brain for something to say — anything.

"So where's your boyfriend? Does he know you're out?"

Her head jerks up. I guess I touched a nerve. "Do I know you?"

"Um . . . no. I mean, a girl like you must have a boyfriend, right?" I'm not about to admit to seeing her on the bus. "So, do you have a boyfriend?"

"Uh — yeah. I guess so." Her eyes are back to staring at her feet.

"Would he be cool if he knew you were out here chilling with some random guy?" I was trying to be funny, but as soon as the words come out, I hear how not funny they are.

"He'd freak out." A slight laugh slips out of her mouth, but it's drenched in contempt.

"Is he . . . the reason you're out here?" She looks at me sharply out of the corner of her eye. Based on the scene on the bus, and my dream, it was a logical guess. She says nothing.

"I mean, if he is . . . aren't there less drastic ways to deal with it? Like maybe just break up with him or something?"

"It's not that simple." She's not agreeing, but at least she said something.

Five or six seconds pass before I can think of anything more to say. Five or six seconds of brutal awkwardness — it feels like a lifetime. Finally I come up with, "I guess not. You must have a ton of crap going on." There's a part of me that just wants to say that it couldn't be that bad. At the same time, a part of me wants to tell her that I get that she feels that way. I get wanting just to die. Weird — something inside me wants to help this girl. I want to help her change her mind. I don't quite get why I care this much.

"There are probably people who might have a really hard time if you . . . you know, weren't around anymore." The hypocrisy bites me again. My parents and sister enter my thoughts.

"What's your name?" I ask.

After two long seconds of silence, she looks up and our eyes meet. "It's Max."

Chapter 11

Help

"I'm Emerson."

I look at the rope in her hands. It's strong enough. But the way her noose is set up, it wouldn't snap her neck. If she was going to die — it would be from choking. It's a far more painful way to go. I wonder if I should bring this up.

"So, what school do you go to?" I ask. If she lives nearby, it's either Riverdale or Malvern. Turns out she goes to Catholic school.

I try to think of other questions I can ask

her. Otherwise we're just going to be standing here in silence. I've decided that I can't just leave her. I think that she must have wanted to talk to someone. Instead of leaving or telling me to screw myself, she's answering my questions.

Max says she should be in university but she's doing a victory lap. This means she's doing grade twelve over again. We're talking now. I ask about her family. She has a little sister, Kim, who's four years younger. I can tell by the way Max mentions her that she's worried about Kim.

"This would be really tough on her, wouldn't it?" I nod toward her rope.

Max is looking down at the ground. She's silent again. It's dark, but I can tell she's starting to cry. "You wouldn't understand." I can barely hear her.

I go out on a limb. "I'm not saying, 'don't do this.' But maybe . . . wait a couple of years . . . until Kim is older." I know this is not the time to have this thought, but I'm pretty proud of this one. I think it's really clever.

And sure enough, she lets out a little laugh. It's mixed with a cough, but I feel like I've just scored a goal.

"You're joking, right?" she says through sniffles. "Postpone killing myself until my little sister gets older?" Her smile is slight, but still — it's a smile.

Now I'm on a roll. "Well, yeah. You know, make the scar as small as possible." After a pause, I suggest that maybe she could consider getting some help. "I know a couple of places you could call." I had read about crisis help lines while doing my research. Some sites suggest calling 911 if you are worried about someone trying to kill themselves. I wonder why we don't learn what to do in this situation at school.

"I don't know what I want to do. I was really going to do this today. I promised myself I was going to. And now, I don't know." She shakes her head.

"Well, if you don't do this now, you still

can tomorrow. But if you *do* do this now, well, that's pretty permanent. Right?"

I decide to tell her about her knot. "Besides, the way you've tied that knot, it's all wrong."

She looks at me like I've got a unicorn horn growing out of my forehead. "Are you serious? You show up out of nowhere and try to talk me off my ledge. And now you're giving advice on how to tie my knot?" She's wearing a look of disbelief, but is kind of smiling too.

I'm speechless. How do I answer this? "Weird, right? I didn't expect to find anyone here." "Why *are* you here?" Max asks.

I remind her that I couldn't sleep. Killing myself isn't going to happen tonight, even if she left right now. I feel like I've got some more thinking to do.

"It's getting cold. How about grabbing a cup of coffee? There's a Tims nearby," I suggest. I expect her to tell me that she's ready to go home, at least for now. But she surprises me.

She nods. "Okay." We start to walk off the bridge. Halfway down the stairs, there's a small landing covered with wet leaves. I feel my feet slip and I fall. As I go down, I accidentally hit Max. She loses her balance and slides right off the landing. She screams as she goes flying off. There's a splash.

Just seconds ago, I talked this girl out of killing herself. Now I've pushed her into the river. I hope to God she knows how to swim, because I don't.

I run down the concrete bank, careful not to fall in. From the landing, she actually didn't have very far to fall. I see her. Max is half sitting and half lying down in shallow water. I remember now that I've seen people wading in this part of the river, fishing.

I trudge into the water to where she is. It is frigid. "Are you okay?" I ask. She tells me that she thinks so, as she reaches for my extended hand. Max yelps in pain as she slowly pulls herself up. She leans on me as we walk out of the river. Her steps are slow.

"If we hadn't just had that talk up there, I'd think you were trying to kill me," she says. I make a face like a mock grin. I feel absolutely horrible for causing her fall. Her limp is bad.

"You should go to the hospital," I say.

"I don't like hospitals." She sits down gingerly and I flop down on the concrete bank. I should have sat more carefully — I think I bruised my tailbone when I fell.

I don't even have to ask her why. "My mother read in my diary that I was thinking about killing myself. I denied it, told her it was just a passing thought. She saw some show on TV about teenage suicides, and the next thing you know, I'm being dragged to the hospital. We waited almost eight hours before seeing a doctor." Her voice has trailed off a bit.

"So what happened at the hospital?" Given what she had come here to do, I suppose she didn't get the help she needed.

"I saw a psychiatrist. The meeting lasted about ten minutes. I wasn't about to kill myself at that moment. They just sent me home." I'd always wondered what would happen to me in that situation.

"You can barely walk. You might've broken a bone, maybe even two. I'll call an ambulance, okay?"

She's shivering. I am too. She tries to get back up and winces in pain. I ask her if I could borrow her phone. I'm a little embarrassed.

I'm grateful she doesn't comment on my not having a phone. I guess you can be forgiven for not having your phone with you if you're out in the middle of the night.

She pulls a cell out of her pocket and hands it to me. I call the ambulance and we sit and wait. Soon enough it arrives, lights flashing, siren turned off. Max is helped onto a stretcher and the two EMS guys carry her up the slope. They place the stretcher on a gurney, the thing with wheels that fold up, and slide her into the ambulance. I lean in to tell Max goodbye. But she asks if I would come along. I don't hesitate and hop right in. I'm wondering what she thinks of me. I tell myself not to be thinking about that right now.

In the ambulance, one of the EMS guys asks us what happened. He asks Max directly if she was trying to kill herself. I'm amazed that he would ask this. I don't say anything — I just look down at her. She is lying flat and wrapped in an orange blanket. At this moment, she starts to cry. The EMS guy tells her that she's going to be okay and then looks over at me. I reach for Max's hand. She lets me hold it, but turns her head away. I can't think of anything to say. We ride the rest of the way to the hospital in silence.

Chapter 12

Surprise

When we get to the hospital, Max is pushed into the ER right up to the triage nurse. We wait quietly for about forty minutes before a nurse comes to tell her that a doctor will see her.

I watch them wheel Max into a room. It's not really a room, but more like a small area contained by a blue curtain. Another really long twenty minutes goes by and she is rolled out again.

"Hey," I say. Nothing is in a cast, but she's in a wheelchair. "Anything broken?"

"Nope. Sprained ankle, some bruises, otherwise as good as new." She smiles.

The triage nurse asks, "Maxine, would you mind sticking around a bit longer? I need you to speak to the psychiatrist before you go."

"I'm okay to go home," Max says.

"It'd work much better if you agreed to see the doctor." Max eventually nods and doesn't argue. We're led to a set of doors under a sign that says *Psychiatric Emergency*. The nurse uses her scan card to unlock the doors. After we're dropped off in the waiting room, I see that she needs to scan her way out again. We're locked in here.

I count seven other people waiting. I look around. They all appear to be here alone. Max turns to me. "Thanks for staying with me, Emerson. They would've called my mom or the police if I didn't agree to stay. They'll probably just send me home after talking to me for a couple minutes."

I smile at her. "I had nothing better to do anyway."

This area is kind of crowded. There are a couple of other girls around our age. There's one guy who looks like he's in his late twenties. He's going on and on about something or other but he's completely incoherent. He seems to know all the staff though, as if he was here on a regular basis. I whisper to Max that I'd never been in a psychiatric ER before. I tell her that it's interesting.

She comes back with, "Easy for you to say." She isn't smiling. Before I can think of a reply, we're interrupted by a different nurse. She explains that soon Max will be seen by a social worker and the resident psychiatrist. She leads us to a small room and leaves us there. We only wait a couple of minutes before there's a knock at the door. It's the social worker. She lets herself in.

The second I see her, I am completely filled with dread. I feel like I've just been caught red-handed trying to steal the world's biggest diamond. I'd never in a million years have thought that the overnight social worker at the hospital might be someone I knew. But she is. And my parents know her too.

It's Joyce, the Chinese customer who comes into our store twice a month. I feel a surge of cold flush through me. My instinct is to get away. Maybe I could just get up and leave? But I'm frozen to my seat. What is Joyce thinking? The boy from the dry cleaners, the son of respectable Chinese elders, shows up at a hospital ER. With a girl. At three in the morning. I have that feeling I get when I know my parents are about to discover one of my fails.

She introduces herself. It erases the tiny bit of hope I was clinging to, that maybe this woman just happens to look exactly like Joyce from the store. She doesn't give any indication that she knows me though. I'm holding my breath. Not on purpose.

Max says hi. Joyce looks down at her clipboard and confirms our names. We nod. If she hadn't realized it was me, there's no way she doesn't know it now. Emerson is an odd enough name that people rarely forget it. They often get it wrong — Everson or Everton. Still, when they hear it, they remember. But Joyce doesn't pay me any special attention.

She starts speaking. "Everything we talk about will be kept confidential. I may discuss your situation with other hospital staff, for the purpose of providing you with the best care possible. But everyone here is bound by the same rules."

Max nods as if she's heard this before. "And because you're both at least sixteen, I would need to get your permission to share anything we talk about with anyone else." Joyce looks at Max first and then at me before continuing. "There are only three exceptions to this rule: If one of you tells me that you're planning to seriously harm a specific person. Or if something you tell me leads me to suspect that someone under the age of sixteen is at risk of harm. Or if your file is subpoenaed by a judge."

She stares straight at me and says, "This means that I will not be talking about you or your situation with anyone I might know outside of the team at the hospital." I feel my shoulders relax. I hadn't realized how tensed up they had been. I thank Joyce inside my head. I think to myself that she would make a pretty good poker player.

Joyce asks Max to please tell her what happened tonight. There is something about the way she speaks that makes you feel like you want to tell her things. I wonder if Max feels this. I look over at her. She doesn't say anything.

Joyce says, "This must be very difficult. Maxine, how can I help you?"

Max's eyes are fixed on the floor. Her voice is very quiet, but she starts to talk.

"I fought with my sister . . . earlier tonight.

She'd taken my shirt and my lipstick without asking." She stops talking. *That's it!? What about your crazy-mean boyfriend?* I had seen and heard how that guy talked to her. *Tell Joyce about him!*

Joyce says, "It sounds like the conflict with your sister is really stressful."

But that wasn't the reason you were on the bridge Max, I think. No one says anything for what feels like forever. There has to be more.

Finally Joyce asks Max, "How have the last couple of days been for you?" Max looks over at me and then her eyes turn back to the floor.

"I saw my father yesterday."

Silence.

"How did that go?" Joyce asks gently.

"I hadn't seen him for almost six months before yesterday. It started out okay but it ended the way it always ends. He wanted money from my mother. But my mother hasn't worked in almost two years." Joyce nods and jots down some notes. "When my mom couldn't give him any money, he got mad. He can be pretty rough." Max gets teary again. I pass her the box of tissue that happened to be on the table next to me. She goes on to say she was furious at her mother. Instead of being relieved that he was gone, her mom has been even more upset and impossible to live with since then.

"Is your mother okay?" Joyce asks.

"She's got a bruise on her face." Max is still looking down at the floor. "Mom is on medication for depression. She just takes this crap from my dad and doesn't do anything about it."

"That's a lot for you to have to deal with, Maxine," Joyce says. She waits for what feels like forever. It was probably barely a minute. "Do you feel like you have to look after your mom?"

"I feel that, with my mom being like that, I should be looking after my sister," Max replies.

"The one who takes your things without asking?"

Max nods. "We fight all the time. She's hanging out with a bad crowd." Max dabs her eyes with a tissue. "I think she's doing a lot of drugs."

"That's certainly a heavy burden for you," Joyce says.

My mind starts to race. This story sounds familiar. She's worried about her kid sister who's doing drugs. She has a violent dad who left the family. Her mother is depressed and on meds. And she's been thinking about killing herself? I look over at Max. Could she be . . . Frmda6?? My head spins.

Chapter 13

Why?

Could I be sitting on the same couch as the online stranger who I poured my heart out to? Could she be the same random girl I'd seen on a bus just yesterday, who also happened to show up in one of my dreams? Frmda6 had a crazy-jealous boyfriend — that must be the guy from the bus! My mind is officially blown!

"Emerson? . . . Emerson?" Joyce's voice shakes me out of my stupor. "Are you okay?" The shock must've shown on my face.

"Sorry. I'm a bit tired," I say. It's not the whole truth, but I'm not lying either.

Max continues and I feel badly for her. For all my parents' faults, they're doing better than Max's family. Dad would never leave us. And they would both do anything and everything to look after me, even if they are totally warped in their thinking.

I like Max. If she really is Frmda6, she is the first person I've ever shared my problems with. I wish she could get through this and somehow be happy. I don't know what to think about my own situation anymore.

Joyce asks Max what she did to cope with all the hard things she's dealing with. Max answers, ". . . Well, I listen to music in my room a lot. I chill with my dog. But I'm sad a lot too."

Joyce tells her, "Music and your dog are good strategies. I think there are other strategies that could be added to your tool box, Maxine." She continues, "Today, you decided to do something far more drastic. Have you thought about or actually tried hurting yourself before?"

Max nods slowly. "I've thought about killing myself for . . . I don't know, a long time, I guess." I watch her face redden. Joyce waits. I feel exhausted. But then Max does something to make me forget how tired I am. Still staring at the floor, she pulls up both her sleeves.

Her forearms have been slashed. There are scars on each side — my head turns away before I can count how many. Max's arms look like they've been created by a makeup artist working on a horror movie. That's the best I can describe it. I wonder for a second if maybe her father or her boyfriend did that to her. Joyce asks her if she'd made those cuts herself. Max nods while she pulls her sleeves back down. I've heard about kids who cut themselves. But I'd never actually seen it before. I feel like throwing up.

Joyce asks, "Max, did the doctor see your

arms earlier?" Max shakes her head. "Would you be okay with a doctor looking over your cuts, when we're done talking? Just to be sure they're not infected." Max nods. I wonder if her mom and dad know about this. Or her boyfriend. Wouldn't that be enough for them to get her some help? Or at least treat her better? She must hide the cuts from everyone. I know if it was me, I would be careful not to show anyone. I felt sick when I saw them, but I'm glad Max decided to show Joyce.

Then Joyce asks about me. "How long have you and Emerson been friends? It's wonderful you had someone to come to the hospital with." I freeze.

Max answers. "We met on the bridge for the first time. Emerson just showed up. If he hadn't come at that exact moment, I might have gone through with it."

"You two didn't know each other before tonight?" Joyce's eyes widen. "What were you doing in the park at that time, Emerson?"

"Uh . . . I couldn't sleep." It helps that I've repeated this excuse a couple of times to Max. I push my backpack farther under my chair with my foot. If anyone found my noose, there would be a lot of explaining to do. "I sometimes go for a ride on my bike when I can't sleep."

"Hmmm . . . does that happen often? Maybe you could talk to a doctor about your sleep issue."

I tell Joyce that I will see my family doctor.

She says, "Okay, please do. It was fortunate that you were out tonight though." She smiles at me and then at Max. Joyce thanks Max for sharing. She asks me if I have anything more to add. I shake my head. Joyce excuses herself and promises to come back shortly with the psychiatrist. As soon as she leaves the room, Max leans her head on my shoulder. I think that this has been a horrible night. But I also feel a little guilty, because I'm kind of feeling happy right now. I know that none of my problems have gone anywhere. And they're really nothing in comparison to Max's problems. But at this moment, none of that matters.

A few minutes later, Joyce comes back with a man who introduces himself as Dr. Singh. Joyce retells Max's story, frequently stopping to ask if she's getting it right and asking Max to correct her if she hasn't. Dr. Singh asks Max how she feels right now and if she has any plans for the next day or two. She shrugs and shakes her head. He tells her that there is a bed available for her at this hospital and that he thinks it would be a good idea for her to stay for a couple of days. After about three long seconds, Max nods. Dr. Singh and Joyce leave, telling Max that a nurse will come and get her in a few minutes. Max looks at me and I search my brain for something to say. "I'm glad that they're not just sending you home." It's all I can come up with.

Then Max kisses me. Her lips press firmly against mine. She closes her eyes and leans her head on my shoulder again. I just sit there, surprised at what just happened. I don't feel the least bit tired anymore, and it feels okay not to say anything.

Chapter 14

Worse

The next morning, I wake up and every single thing that happened last night replays in my head like a movie. I lie on my bed and go through the scene again, the few moments just before the nurse took Max up to her ward. I check the time. It's nine. I've slept for almost four hours. My parents must've left for the store already. They didn't even try waking me up. Strange. Normally, my parents doing something like this would cause me to worry.

But all I can think about is what Max said just before I left her: "Find me on Facebook."

I go downstairs and jump on the computer. I try logging onto my Facebook account and it's still inactive. I sigh and shake my head. I'm so annoyed — but whatever. I set up a new email address so I can set up a new account in Facebook. I find Max and send her a friend request. I stare at the little *find friends* icon. Nothing. Another second passes by. Still nothing. I refresh the page. I tell myself to calm down.

There it is. She's accepted my request.

She messages me. It's a comment about the fact that my page is entirely empty — no profile pic, no photos, no friends. She asks me if I just came onto Facebook for the first time ever. I respond by saying:

Me: Any chance u remember what happened to Frmda62? I mean what he told you happened to his FB account?

Max: ????????????????!!!!!!!!!!!!!!!!!!!!!!!!!!!!!

Me: . . . so u ARE frmda6?

Max: Em, how the hell did you find me last night??

Me: That was just a coincidence. I didn't 'find' u —
just a crazy coincidence. I didn't even have a clue it
was you until I heard you tell ur story 2 Joyce @ the
hospital.

There's no response for like over an entire
minute. I type and ask if she's still there.

Max: Yeah. I just . . . Wow!

There's a pause.

Max: So, tell me again — what were you doing at
the park at that hour?

Me: Let's just say there's still some rope in my backpack.

Max: NO!!! Hey! You should be in this hospital with me!

Me: What's it like in there?

She tells me about the other patients in the ward. There are seven others, a real mix of older and young people, both men and women. She has to do some kind of group session with them later, so she will probably get to know them a little bit.

Then she suddenly remembers my problems as Frmda62. She messages me about stories she had read on a website about how people tracked down their lost phones. The site is called Reddit and she embeds a link in the message. Reddit acts like a community bulletin board where people post all kinds of stuff, including questions relating to just about anything. I click on the link, and I see a story from a girl in New Jersey who asked readers for help locating her lost phone. She got a ton of advice about tracking apps. She got her phone back!

Max asks me if I have a cell phone tracking GPS app on my phone. I don't. I went online the night the police came to the house and tried to track my phone using the suggestions I found on my wireless provider's website — but they were useless. She asks me if my phone was connected to any cloud storage. Some guy in California found his phone because pictures the thief took of himself using the phone were automatically uploaded to the owner's cloud account. He used clues from the pictures to track down the thief. If whoever has my phone takes any pictures using the cell, it might help me find out where they are. I tell Max that I will go look.

My phone is connected to service called Lockbox. It automatically backs up my phone with any changes I make in my contacts, photo gallery or even my phone log. It takes a couple of seconds to log in. I whisper the word "please" out loud.

There are a bunch of pictures that have been uploaded since my phone went missing. I recognize the pictures that were used in the fake Facebook posts: the yearbook pictures of my VP and Ms. McAdam and one of the gun. There are a couple of pics of two guys posing with the gun.

Max messages me:

Any luck?

I let her know.

Awesome! Any clues you can use?

The excitement I felt when I discovered the pictures is starting to fade. The pictures of the guys were taken at night, so it's dark. They were shot from a balcony, and judging from what I can see in the background, it looks like they're on the second floor. I can just make out some of the storefronts across the street, but not any of the words on the signs. I squint to try to figure out the pictures on the signs. They're blurry, but the one that is the clearest looks like an animal of some sort. A buffalo maybe? The store next to that one has a stick figure person on the sign.

I Google Image search "buffalo." Of course I get a billion unrelated images of buffaloes. I try "buffalo store" and "buffalo restaurant" — more useless hits. I give Max the bad news. A bunch of pictures. Two guys. Some blurry signs. Nothing of any use.

"It's okay," she writes. She instructs me to post the pictures on Reddit and ask people if they recognize the signs. She tells me to write about what happened. People love to help out if someone's been badly wronged.

I follow her instructions. It feels like a total long shot, but I guess I have nothing to lose. It takes me almost thirty minutes to create an

account, upload the pics and write my story.
Now I guess I wait.

I message Max again.

Me: So how are you really doing in there?

Max: *shrug*

Me: Talk to any1 from home?

Max: Spoke to my mom. Kim's coming by later.

I take this to mean that her mother won't
be visiting. If it were me in the hospital, my
parents would be worried out of their minds.
You wouldn't even be able to keep my parents
away with all the security in the world. It drives
me crazy, but I guess it's better than them not
caring. I feel bad for Max.

Me: That's great.

Max: Keep me posted on what happens with Reddit.

I look through Max's pages on Facebook. She has almost a thousand friends, three times as many as I had on my old account. Most of the pics are of her and her girlfriends. For someone who's had it so rough for the past six months or longer, she doesn't have the usual dark or moody posts that you see on so many girls' walls. Just based on what you see of her online, you'd think she was doing fine. I do notice that sometimes there are gaps in the posts, a month here, a month and a half there. In almost all the photos, she's wearing long sleeves. I probably wouldn't have even noticed that if it weren't for what I saw at the hospital yesterday.

I check the Reddit page. There are already two responses! I'm excited, until I read the comments. Two people tell me that my "situation sucks" and to "hang in there." I surf aimlessly on the net. I come across a story on Yahoo about a post that has gone viral on Instagram. It's a picture of two graves with two heads superimposed onto the tombstones. One is VP Selvadurai and the other is Ms. McAdam. Mr. S is wearing a turban and Ms. McAdam is wearing a hijab. The picture's been photoshopped very poorly. There are black Xs where their eyes should be. The caption reads:

MCI students stay home tomorrow — You've been warned.

The short blurb states that this picture showed up on Instagram from the account of Emerson Yeung and that police are investigating. The home phone rings, startling me. I check the call display. It's the Toronto police.

Chapter 15

Go Look

I don't answer the phone. I pull on a baseball cap and grab my sunglasses. I take my parents' laptop from their room. Alice and I bought this for them a year ago, so they could stream movies at the store during quiet periods. But they refused to get Internet at the store and have hardly ever touched it. I shove it into my backpack. I shoot out the door and jump on my bike. As I ride away, I think I can hear a police siren in the distance. I ride straight to the public library three blocks from my house. I circle to the rear of the building. This was the first place I could think of that was close enough, safe and connected.

I'm relieved that no one else is here. I pull out the laptop and log into the library's Wi-Fi. I wonder to myself if I'm being too paranoid, but I can't help feeling nervous. If I could just get my phone back, I figure I can clear all this up. I pull up the photo again. I stare at the blurry picture of the sign with the animal and try to figure out what the hell it is. There's a part there that's hidden from view by a lamp post. I open a browser and try Googling "black sign" and "restaurant" with "east end Toronto" and "Scarborough" and "beaches." I get a billion hits — and not one that is helpful.

I try Reddit again. My heart starts to beat a little quicker when I see that there is now a slew of new posts responding to my original question. I skim through a bunch of posts that don't offer anything useful — lots of comments though about the photo. Some people have come across the Instagram post too. Finally I see an answer that says the animal on the sign is a bear. Then there is another post, a few responses down, that says it's the Black Bear Pub. I Google "Black Bear Pub" and get a hit in the east end of Toronto! Google even gives me an address. I search Google maps, find the location and then go to street view. *BINGO!* It looks just like the sign from the picture. This is crazy, but some Reddit users have identified where the picture was taken.

I don't know if I should take this information to the police. They're the freaking police — why haven't they been able to track down my phone? And now I'm running and hiding from them. How wrong is this? I feel a rush. I'm not a bit tired despite not having slept much in days.

I open the photo of the restaurant sign and take in every detail. I check the map again to make sure I know how to get there from the library. I'm about twelve blocks away. I memorize the route. I throw the laptop back into my backpack and cycle off. My chest starts to hurt a little — my heart is pounding against it from the inside. I'm not sure exactly what the plan is when I get there. Hoping that those guys are out in the street in front of the apartment where they happened to take a picture two nights ago is beyond stupid. But since I don't have any better ideas, I keep cycling.

As I ride, I see a police car stopped at a red light. I do a U-turn and detour a block west. There's no chance that the entire Toronto police department is out looking for me. I argue with myself that it doesn't hurt to be safe. I start checking in each direction around me every few seconds. I see another police car behind me and I'm instantly afraid. I turn right and then immediately left. I'm riding up an alley. I repeat under my breath over and over, *please don't let them follow me.* I look over my shoulder and there's no one there. I remember to breathe.

Finally, I pull up in front of the Black Bear Pub. This is crazy! There's a pizza place next door, with a stick figure delivery guy on its sign. I look up and down the street. There are a couple of cars driving up in my direction, but no police. Across the street from the pub is another plaza with a bunch of storefronts and a single storey of apartment units sitting atop the shops. They must live in one of these apartments. There are a total of sixteen units on either side. We used to live in one like this for a while before we moved into our house — it was above the dry cleaners.

Based on the angle of the picture, I try to figure out which unit they shot the picture from. These places usually have their entrances through a door in between two stores with staircases leading up. But here, there are no extra doors along the storefronts. Maybe the entrances are in the back. I cycle to the end of one building. There is a door on the side, with a panel of buzzers. A lady comes out, startling me. I drop my bike and grab a hold of the door. I have to move quickly to catch it before it closes, in case it's the kind that automatically locks. The lady looks at me funny, but then just walks away. I'm a seventeen-year-old wearing a hoodie, out in the middle of the day. But I glance up and down the road again and I see another person who pretty much fits my description. This is a fairly common look.

I carefully place my backpack to act like a doorstop and lock up my bike. How stupid would it be if I was careless and let my bike get stolen? My heart is still hammering away in my chest. I look at the list of names next to the buzzer buttons. I don't know what I'm looking for. I climb the stairs. Am I just going to go door to door? I'll knock and then say what? *Excuse me, but by any chance have you stolen my phone?* When I get to the top, I'm standing in a long hallway with ratty orange carpeting. There are stains scattered along the entire length of the hall. There are cobwebs on the upper corners and the walls are dirty too.

My heart is racing and I feel light-headed. I knock on the first door. No answer. I'm partially relieved. Second door, no answer. Third door, same thing. I wonder if I should skip the fourth door. I stare at the number four hanging from a small nail. My mother is over the top when it comes to avoiding the number four. Apparently, in Chinese culture, it represents death.

When I was little, my parents signed me up for house league soccer. I remember going to meet the coach and pick up my uniform. We were one of the first families to get there, so I pretty much had my choice of numbers. I wanted the number four. It was only because I was four years old at the time. I guess I was too young to have any other system for choosing numbers. I was a stubborn kid, so I freaked out when my mother told me to pick any other number. Then, of course, my dad flipped out at me for making a scene. I almost didn't get to play soccer that year. I was allowed to play only because I calmed down. My parents stayed adamant until the end. Who does that? I guess they thought it was a way of protecting me. I wore the number five.

I knock. A woman about my mom's age opens the door. She's wearing a one-piece body suit with a leopard print.

"Um, I've lost my cell phone and was wondering if maybe someone here might have found it." I do my best to describe what I remember from the picture of the guys in the photos.

"I live here with my husband, and he's no young guy. Sorry, fella," she says. And she closes the door, leaving me standing in this hallway.

This is crazy. I'm not even 100 per cent sure the sign on the Black Bear Pub is the same as the one in the picture. Part of me is relieved though. I'm probably stupid to think that even if I do find the guys, they would just hand over the phone. But now what am I going to do?

There's still the issue with the police threats and the Instagram picture.

I start to leave. Just then, a door opens. I'm standing face to face with one of the guys in the pictures on my phone. He's just come out of unit number five.

Chapter 16

My Phone

I freeze. He's wearing a grey sweatshirt and a Lakers cap. He looks much bigger than I thought he was from the picture. He's easily over six feet tall and 250 pounds. I guess I'm staring at him, because he stares back. He looks at me for a full second and then opens his mouth. "Can I help you?" I feel the words hit me in the face.

I get out an "uh" before I see his eyes grow huge under his shades.

"How did you find us?" He gets really close as he says this, his face right up in mine. I feel a tiny bit of spit hit my cheek. Before I can think of something to say, he grabs a fistful of my shirt at the shoulder and drags me into his apartment.

There's a big screen TV against one wall with an Xbox attached to it. In front of the TV, there's a cluttered coffee table and a couch. There's a table off to the side in front of the tiny kitchen. Around the table are three chairs that don't match each other or the table. The appliances are yellowy-beige like the ones from our first apartment in Canada. There's a hallway with a row of three doors. They must lead to a bathroom and maybe bedrooms or a closet.

"Rob, come check this out!" the guy shouts toward the hallway.

"I thought you were going out to pick up cigarettes, Dennis!" someone shouts out from another room. The other guy from the pictures walks out. Rob, I guess. He is not nearly as big as the first guy, Dennis. Still, he's taller than me and he is totally ripped. He could be a body-double for Tony Jaa.

"Whoa! You're the guy from the phone. Ellerton, Emerton, some weird shit like that, right?" It dawns on me. They would have seen my picture on my Facebook and Instagram accounts.

"Uh . . . my name is Emerson. I came to get my phone back." I barely manage to get the words out.

"I don't know how you did it, but I have to admit I'm impressed China-man. You're the first guy ever to come looking for one of these." Dennis waves his arm at the coffee table. Amidst the mess there are a bunch of cell phones. I notice a few MCI yearbooks too. The China-man comment pisses me off. Now I'm mad and nervous at the same time.

Rob asks, "Dennis, where'd you find this guy?"

"He was right outside. I guess he found us!" Dennis answers.

Rob looks at me and asks, "How the hell did you do that?"

"Yeah, how the hell *did* you find us?" Dennis repeats.

"Never mind how I found you. Just give me my phone back," I say. I have to make an effort to breathe. I didn't expect to be this nervous. I'm trying to work out in my head what I'm going to do. What if these guys refuse to give me my phone back? I've got nothing.

"You can't just walk in here demanding shit that's not yours," Dennis says.

"The phone *is* mine. You know that." I tell myself that I can do this. I look right into his eyes. "Give it to me." I push the words out.

"I don't think you understand. Didn't they teach you in school how the law works? Possession is nine-tenths of the law. I have possession of this here phone." He pulls a phone out of his pocket. It looks like mine. "That means this belongs to me, son."

Then he puts his hand up, the one not

holding the phone, and moves to push my chest. I wait till his hand is about to touch me, and then I step back. He stumbles forward.

I used to get into fights when I was eight or nine. There were these kids in my neighbourhood who picked on other kids. I was a regular target of this group, for no reason I could figure out, other than being Chinese. So I was forced to fight. The first couple of times, I came home pretty bruised and scratched up.

My dad tried to teach me how to fight. But when you're eight or nine, fighting is mostly lots of pushing each other back and forth until someone falls. Then the other guy jumps on top and you wrestle until someone starts crying. The one who's not crying pretty much declares himself the winner. The one trick I did learn from my father was not to resist the force from someone else. It was more effective if you moved with your opponent in the same direction. The other guy would expect the opposite and, as a result, lose his balance. It was probably the only time my dad ever took my side in an argument with my mother. Her solution was for me to practise running as fast as I could to get out of these situations.

I think I'm being smart, making him stumble, but the move backfires. When Dennis almost falls, Rob has a big laugh. This ticks Dennis off. He gathers himself and swears at me. Then without any warning, he tackles me football style. We go flying and smash into the wall. I crumple to the floor and he lands on top of me. I have trouble breathing — this guy is a truck. He takes his time climbing off me. I'm still on the floor when he pretends to dust his hands off, and then out of nowhere, he kicks me in my side. I clutch my midsection. I hear him chuckle. My head spins a little — I wonder how I'm going to get out of here.

I lean against the wall and pull myself to my feet. My side feels like it's just been hit by a wrecking ball. The pain is worse than anything I've ever experienced before. How can I use my head to get out of this? My muscles just aren't going to get the job done here. Forget the phone. I have to get out and get the police. I'm sure that I have a bruise bad enough to justify going after these guys even if the cops don't care about my phone being here. And then, as if I wasn't already terrified, Dennis pulls something out of his pocket. It's a knife in a sheath.

Rob draws my attention by making a *tsk tsk tsk* sound. "You're really not too smart, are you, Everson? It's just a cell phone. But you go to all the trouble of tracking it down and you come here by yourself? Where are your boys, brother? You've got to bring backup to a showdown like this. And then to top it off, you piss poor Dennis off with your little dodgeball move."

Dennis pulls the knife out. The blade is about five inches long.

In this instant, my head fills with all the thoughts and memories of the last couple of days. What if Max hadn't been in the park? Would I have gone through with it? I realize that I haven't thought about killing myself for the past forty-eight hours. I'm sure now that I don't want to die. Not now.

Dennis's voice seems even deeper now as he says to me, "I need to be sure that you don't go to the police, China-man."

The sunlight through the window bounces blindingly off the blade of Dennis's knife. I think to myself how ironic it would be if I did die now after all.

Chapter 17

Fight

Over the years, I've argued with my parents about a lot of things. When I was little, I wanted to play hockey like all my friends. My mother thought it was too dangerous. I thought my dad would back me up because he liked to watch Maple Leaf games on TV. But instead he gave me some crap that playing hockey took up too much time and would distract me from school. By then I'd already overheard my parents talking about the cost of putting a kid in hockey. They let me play soccer instead, which was much cheaper. In those early years, money was a big worry for them. In the end, I played soccer for eight years. At this moment, I wish it had been boxing or tae kwon do.

Dennis waves the knife from side to side. His knees are slightly bent. He looks ready to cut me.

I guess this is better than him pulling his gun. I figure I can try to fight, or I can make a break for it and just run for the door. My side is still throbbing from being kicked. My hands are shaking. I feel a bead of sweat drop from my temple. I'm in no shape to fight. I'm leaning heavily against the wall farthest from the exit. My backpack is on the floor maybe three metres away. Dennis is between me and the door. Rob is sitting on the arm of the couch, watching.

I notice I'm breathing faster.

Rob says, "What are you waiting for, Dennis?"

Dennis takes a step forward. I scream at the top of my lungs, hoping just to confuse him. I move to my left and the table blocks Dennis's route toward me.

I bolt. And I trip. I fall toward Rob. We both end up on the couch — me on top of him. Now Dennis is the one screaming. I turn my head to look toward him. He's charging at us with his knife held high. He leaps into the air and dives toward me. I close my eyes and try to roll out of the way. I fall off the couch.

Rob lets out a shriek. "You bitch! You stabbed me!"

Rob is pushing Dennis off him. His shirt is a dark mess of red and black. It looks like he's been stabbed where his shoulder meets his chest. Dennis is standing next to him holding the knife.

"Look at what you made me do," Dennis says to me. It looks like his face is about to explode.

I break to my right to get around the couch. I reach for my backpack. My phone has fallen to the floor too — I grab it. Dennis darts around the other side and is closer to the exit door than I am. I'm not going to make it out. Instead I head into their hallway and jump into the first room. It's the bathroom. I try to slam the door shut, but Dennis is right there, pushing it open. I lunge with my all my body weight, ignoring the pain in my side. The door closes and I quickly turn the little knob to lock it. I feel Dennis slam his body against the door.

He yells, "Open the door, you little bitch!" My breathing is so fast now I worry I might pass out.

Rob yells for help.

It sounds like Dennis has gone to him. It feels good to have my phone in my hand again. I press a button and the screen lights up. Of course the phone doesn't have any service and the battery is only at 5 per cent power. I remember hearing somewhere that cell phones can dial 911 whether they have service or not. I don't know if this is true, but I'm about to find out. *Please work.* 9.1.1. It doesn't even ring. Then someone comes on.

"Emergency services — Police, Fire or EMS?"

I explain that I'm trapped in a bathroom and I need the police. The call gets transferred to the police department. A new voice asks how she can help so I repeat myself. She asks me if I'm being held against my will. I say "yes." She asks me if I know my captors. I say "no." Then she asks me if they have broken into my home. We go back and forth like this:

Me: I'm not at home. This is probably their place.

Dispatcher: You're in their home?

Me: Yes. It's a long story. Please send the police. And maybe an ambulance too.

Dispatcher: Are you hurt?

Me: Well, yeah. But the ambulance is for someone else. Someone's been stabbed.

Dispatcher: Someone's been stabbed?

Me: Yes! Someone's been stabbed!

Dispatcher: Who has been stabbed and by whom?

Me: One of the guys who stole my phone stabbed the other guy.

Dispatcher: You are being held against your will by captors. But you are in *their* apartment. And one of the captors has stabbed the other captor? Are you aware that it's a criminal offense to prank call 911?

Me: This isn't a prank! The guy out there is going to kill me!

Dennis is now back banging on the door and yelling for me to come out. He's loud enough that the woman on the phone can hear.

Dispatcher: Is that them trying to get at you?

Me: Yes! Please send the police already!

Finally she asks what the address is. She seems annoyed that I don't know the postal code. I'm surprised that I can even remember the street address.

Dennis is still banging and yelling. "Who are you talking to?!"

She asks me a bunch of questions, like my birthday and my home address. When I tell her I'm seventeen, she asks for my parents' names and their phone number. I tell her. She asks me what I was doing here. The phone's been beeping since I picked it up. It beeps again and goes dead. The battery's toast. I look around to see if maybe there's another phone. No luck. Dennis is slamming his body against the door, trying to knock it down. One of the hinges rips right out of the wall. I try to open the small window but it's jammed shut. I look for something to smash it with. Then I hear sirens.

Please, please be coming here.

Chapter 18

Lucky

The sirens get louder. They must be getting closer. I'm sure now that there is more than one police car.

"Shit!" Dennis sounds panicked. I look out the window. Behind the building, there is a strip of parking spots but no police cars. I hear Rob and Dennis yelling and swearing at each other. There is some scrambling. It sounds like they leave in a hurry.

I unlock the door and open it slowly. As

I step out of the bathroom, two police officers enter the apartment with their guns drawn. My arms shoot up. I recognize one of them. He's Constable Williams — the one who came to my house two days ago about the Facebook threats. I never thought I'd be this happy to see him.

"I thought the name sounded familiar," he says, lowering his gun. He gestures to the other cop to put his gun away.

"Are you hurt? EMS is downstairs. Need any help getting down?"

I say, "I'm okay. I think I can manage." Constable Williams radios someone outside and lets them know that we're heading down.

As we leave the apartment, a couple of people in uniforms carrying tool boxes hurry inside. Outside, the parking strip at the front of the building has grown full. There are four police cruisers and two ambulances. I see Dennis in the back seat of one of the cruisers. Rob is being loaded into one of the ambulances on a folding gurney.

I'm led to the other ambulance. The EMS woman introduces herself — Jill. She asks me what happened. I give her a rundown of the fight, highlighting the kick to my side, being tackled and getting crushed by the 250-pound behemoth. She asks me a bunch of questions — checking for a concussion. There's another EMS person and two cops watching. I feel like I'm on display. I wish they'd go and do something else.

Jill checks out my side. It's very red. She asks me to lift my arm. When I do, I feel a sharp pang. There's pain too when I take a deep breath in, but it's not as sharp.

"You have a contusion on your ribs," Jill says. "That's just a fancy way of saying that they're bruised. You're really lucky. It could have been much worse."

As soon as she says "worse" my parents' car pulls up. At least I can tell them that there's nothing wrong with me medically.

Mom runs over to me. I try to remember the last time I saw her run.

She asks, "Are you okay?"

"I'm fine," I tell her, and she starts to cry. She puts her arms around my neck and pulls me into her. Mom never cries. I struggle to remember the last time I saw her cry too. She gets upset often enough, especially when my dad is mean to her. But she always holds it in. The last time I know she cried was four years ago — when we got word from China that my grandmother had died after a heart attack. My mother hadn't seen her since our move to Canada. Even then, she stayed in her room for about six straight hours. I heard her weeping quietly through the closed door. Seeing her cry right now, I realize just how worried she must have been. I'm sure that I'm going to pay later for making her feel this way.

She keeps hugging me. The last hug I can remember getting from her was when I was valedictorian for my grade eight class. It wasn't really a hug then. She just put her arm around my shoulder. I lean into her. "Mom, I'm good.

Really." I look up and my father is now standing with us.

"Maybe you should go to the hospital?" Dad asks. I tell him that the EMS woman said I was okay. He sighs. The only thing showing on his face is relief.

Constable Williams tells us that I have to come into the police station to answer questions and give a statement. I feel dread wash over me as I get in our car. I can already hear them asking me how I could be so stupid. Why I would put myself in such a dangerous situation. All the doors slam shut and Dad pulls away. There is dead silence in the car.

We drive two whole blocks before anyone says anything. Then Mom turns to me from the front passenger seat and asks again if I'm okay. I nod and see my dad peek at me in the rear-view mirror. That's all that's said during the entire ten minutes it takes to get to the police station. No questions about whether I was happy to bring them one step closer to their graves with the worry I caused. It seems like forever since I last saw them, when I split from the store. I don't know what to think.

I get out of the car with Mom. She insists on staying with me. My father goes back to the store. We meet Constable Williams inside and he guides us into an interview room. He tells us that they found a gun and ammunition in Dennis and Rob's apartment.

"It matches the one from the Facebook post, Emerson," he explains. "It appears that they're both former students from MCI. Do you know them?"

"They looked familiar, but I don't know them," I answer.

He suggests that they stole my phone and then figured out what school I went to from my social media. "They likely saw it as a chance to screw with the vice principal and one of the teachers. We'll know more as we complete the investigation."

Then Constable Williams calls in another

officer who is an expert on social-media-related crimes. She gives me some advice on what to do about the Instagram picture. She tells me to go through every social-media account I have. She explains what I have to do to minimize the damage and to maximize security.

Constable Williams tells us that the forensics department will work hard to go through the evidence. If what I've told him is true, within a week or two, I'd be done as far as any charges were concerned. "For what it's worth, Emerson, I believe your story," he says.

I say that I'm glad it's finally over. He informs me that it isn't completely. I will be asked to testify against Dennis and Rob. For that, I will have to appear in court. I ask if I can have my phone back. Constable Williams tells me that it's currently police evidence. After the case is done, I can apply to have it returned. It will likely take a year or two.

"Seriously?!" I cannot believe my ears. And after everything I just went through.

"I'm glad things worked out, Emerson. But things could have turned out much differently." He's in lecture mode. "What you did was very dangerous. A boy your age was killed not too long ago, trying to do exactly what you did today. Do you understand?" I guess he's obligated to point out the obvious.

I nod.

Constable Williams offers us a ride home. I was thinking we would have to take the bus back to our store. My parents never take a cab anywhere and I didn't expect the kind gesture from the police. My mom thanks him, but declines. She says that she is very grateful to the police for saving my life. They are too busy to be chauffeuring us around as well. I swallow a groan. I was still in pain, kind of tired and would have really appreciated the lift. But I guess it's the bus.

Mom thanks Constable Williams again and we head toward the exit. As we walk, she calls my dad on the flip phone to let him know that we are finally done. I turn in the direction of the bus stop. Mom holds me back by my arm. She tells me that we are going to wait for my dad to pick us up.

"Dad's closing the store again to pick us up?" I can't believe this.

"Yes," Mom answers.

Chapter 19

Swiss Chalet

"He wants to take you somewhere to eat" is the explanation for Dad's reappearance at the police station.

The two questions my parents ask me the most often are, "Shouldn't you be studying?" and "Did you eat?" One time I ordered pizza at one in the morning. My dad was out of bed to go to the bathroom when the delivery guy arrived. I thought, *Crap! I'm in trouble.* But because I was up studying and I was getting food, much to my surprise, Dad was cool with it. It's crazy enough that my dad would close the store when he didn't have to. But we never eat out. To my parents, it's a waste of money to go to a restaurant when "you can make the same food at home for less than half the cost." I'm beginning to wonder if I'd hit my head during my fight with Dennis. Is this really happening?

My dad takes us to Swiss Chalet for chicken. I smile as he drives into the parking lot. I'm sure the only reason my father even knows that this is a restaurant is because he's seen the ads on TV. I wonder if he's secretly wanted to try the food here but could never admit it because of his philosophy about eating out.

We are waiting for our food when Mom says, "You are lucky to still be alive."

Then my dad says in Chinese, "*We* are lucky that you are still alive." I couldn't have heard that right. I ask my mom to translate what he said to be sure I understood. Before she can answer, Dad puts his hand on my shoulder. He says in English, "Emerson, we very lucky you are alive." His eyes are welling up but he doesn't try to hide it.

My eyes well up too, causing me to laugh, because for our family, this scene is simply bizarre. Both of my parents laugh as well.

"Emerson, often parents are the last ones to see when their children have grown up. I have not made an effort to see things from your side." He is back to speaking Chinese, and being careful to use words that he knows I understand. "I thought I was trying my best to be a good father, but maybe I can try harder."

Mom explains further. "Emerson, your father is trying to say that he is sorry if we are too harsh with you. I know it doesn't look that way to you, but he is trying to be a good father."

The waitress places a bunch of dishes in front of us. Dad picks up the little bowl with water and lemon in it. He asks, "This is the tea?"

"It's for your fingers, Dad," I explain. "You can use your hands here to eat the chicken."

Dad smiles and says, "I was worried about having to use a knife and fork." He only ever uses chopsticks.

When we've finished our chicken, Mom pulls out a small box from her purse and places it on the table. My dad picks it up and gives it to me. It's a new cell phone. I knew they'd want me to have a phone so they can get a hold of me at any time. But I didn't expect them to pay for a new one.

"We didn't think you would find your phone. And it looks like you're not going to get it back soon," Mom says.

"Thanks. I'm sorry for losing the first one you bought me. I was going to use my savings to buy a new one. I can pay for this."

"You work in the store on weekends. Let's say that the money we've saved on hiring help went to buying this phone. You hold on to your savings."

In one afternoon, my parents have become different people.

"Go ahead. The boy at the store said it is charged, and by now the service should be on," Mom says.

I know there is no point in arguing with them. I smile and thank them again. Nothing will ever surprise me again.

Chapter 20

Max

After we eat, we head home. My mother wants me to close all my social-media accounts. I agree to at least think about it. I hardly ever use any of them anyway. I just don't like being *told* that I *have* to. Anyway, I will at least make sure my security settings are the way the social-media police specialist said they should be. I turn on the family computer. I secretly hope to find a message from Max. I log in to my new Facebook account. There's one message. It's short.

Hope your search goes well. Be safe.

I message her back.

Just got in. Found my cell but the police are
holding it. How are things with you?

As I wait for a reply, I wonder if they
have her sitting in group therapy or seeing a
counsellor. That's probably it. I decide to head
down to the hospital. I can't wait to tell her
about everything that happened on my search
for the phone.

I tell my parents that a friend is in the
hospital and that I'm heading over to visit her.

Mom looks horrified. "How can you leave
this house after all you went through? And
besides, you need to be studying." She reminds
me I've already missed two days of school. "You
must be so far behind."

I let her know that I can call the school
tomorrow to request work from my teachers.

My dad pipes up, telling my mother just to let me go. I look closely at my dad to gauge the spirit of his permission. Is he cool with me going? Or is this a manipulation? Is he saying I can go but expecting me to do the opposite? He looks at me and tells me not to stay out too long.

* * *

At the hospital, I pop into the gift shop. I'd like to get Max something. A magazine? I have no idea what she's into. Flowers? That might make her feel awkward. Too much like boyfriend/girlfriend. Stuffed animal? It's $25 for a small bear — really? I settle on a small collection of junk food: a few chocolate bars, sour candy, fuzzy peaches and licorice. It's less formal than a box of chocolate. And who wouldn't like all this?

I take the elevator up to the right floor. As I near her room, I hear her voice. She's talking to a guy. She asks him to leave. She calls him Nico.

I stop right outside the door. I hear him tell her that she can't do this to him. I don't know what he means by "this" but he sounds really pissed. I wonder if I should turn around and leave. I should give them some privacy.

Max asks Nico again to leave. I peek in. It's him, the guy from the bus, that first time I saw Max. I argue with myself.

You have to go in.

What if Max doesn't want me to?

You always hesitate at times like this. Just do it.

That guy is much bigger than me.

You're in a hospital. If you get hurt, there are doctors right here. And besides, you're not going in to fight the guy. This can't be stupider than getting trapped in an apartment with knife-carrying phone thieves.

I win the argument.

I knock on the open door twice and walk right in. "Hi, Max," I say in the most normal voice I can manage.

Nico is standing. He looks at me. He turns

to Max and says, "Who the hell is this guy?"

Max looks surprised to see me. She says hi.

Nico turns to me. "Who the hell are you?" He takes a step in my direction.

"I'm Max's friend," I say, remembering to breathe.

Max stands up from her bed. "Listen, Nico. You need to go. Now." Her voice is stronger than it was before.

Nico looks at me and looks back at her. He moves right in front of me, clearly trying to intimidate me. "If you're really Max's friend, you'll leave right now."

Max pushes herself in between us, facing him. "Nico. Don't. If you don't leave now, I'll call the nurse."

Nico fires back, "And what's the nurse going to do?"

Max doesn't move or say anything else. She just stares right into his eyes.

He finally steps back and grabs his jacket from the chair next to the bed. He shakes his head in disgust. Max stands her ground. I do too. He mutters something rude as he leaves.

Max climbs back onto the bed. She has tears in her eyes, so I pass her the tissues from the bedside table. She says that she's sorry about what just happened. Then I surprise myself by crawling up beside her and giving her a hug. She leans into me. I ask her how she's doing and she just shrugs.

"Do you want some chocolate?" I ask, breaking out the bag of goodies.

Max lets a laugh escape and says, "I so need this."

She has big dark purple rings under her eyes. I'm sure she still has a ton of things to work through. I'm hopeful that the staff here will hook her up with the right kind of help. I plan on supporting her in whatever way I can.

"So how's the food here?" I ask.

"The meat is too salty and everything else is bland. You'd think at a hospital the food would be healthier."

"And they serve a lot of jello, right?"

"Yeah. But I really like jello."

"Me too — especially purple."

"I broke up with him — Nico." Max has a satisfied look on her face.

"For what it's worth, I think you can do better." Then I search my brain for something else to say. I remember her telling Joyce about her dog.

"Your dog — what kind is it?"

"Sheriff? He's a pug." She shows me pictures on her phone of her and her sister horsing around with Sheriff. Max's mood lightens a bit. Then her eyes widen like she's just remembered something. "What happened with your phone?"

I give her all the details about using Reddit to find Rob and Dennis's apartment, and the fight, and the stabbing and police. She shakes her head when she hears that the whole thing was over a race issue. "That's really messed that he pulled a knife on you. Are you okay?"

I nod. "When that happened, I thought that I might actually die. Funny thing was, it was exactly in that moment that I knew I didn't want to. It wasn't like my life was any better than when I was thinking about killing myself, but when it was there, right in my face, I knew I didn't want that."

Max puts her hand on mine. "Do your parents know what happened?"

I say, "The police called them. They're the craziest part of this whole thing. They didn't freak out, Max. They *always* freak out. But instead, my dad took us out to eat." Max smiles. "You know, the only times we've ever eaten in a restaurant were when we've had visitors from out of town. My family had never eaten out together before today, ever."

Max leans her head on my shoulder, like the time in the waiting room. I ask her how she's doing. She says that she feels a whole lot better than she did even an hour ago.

We keep talking. It's like we've known each

other for ages. After a while, I check my new phone and two hours have passed since I got here. I give in to the nagging feeling I have — I need to get home. I tell Max that I don't like the idea of leaving her alone. She says, "I'm probably going home tomorrow. We should hang out." She puts her hand on my cheek, smiles and thanks me for coming to see her.

As I pedal quickly toward home, I think that I should have been the one to thank Max. It felt really good to talk to her. It was like eating a really good meal when you're starving, or stepping into a warm room full of light when you've been outside in the dark dead of winter.

I wonder if my parents have started to worry yet. What will their mood be when I get there? I don't know what to expect from them anymore. What would they do if they knew about my plans for the night on the bridge? How would they react if they found out that I spend hours and hours down at the beach in the middle of the night because I can't sleep?

Before today, I would never have thought to talk to anyone about these things. Especially not my parents. But now I'm not ruling it out. I won't just start spilling everything to them all at once. But at least now, it's not that I can't. Or maybe I'll try talking to Joyce first. And now I know that Max will be around too. Suddenly I feel tired. I'm looking forward to getting to bed and getting some sleep tonight.

A Note from the Author

Feeling stressed is an experience most young people have at some point. If you're feeling overwhelmed by school, issues with your family or friends or anything else — try talking to someone you trust. It could be a friend, parent or teacher. You can also get confidential help from a counsellor. To speak to a counsellor right now, call Kids Help Phone at 1-800-668-6868. Kidshelpphone.ca also has lots of useful information.

Acknowledgements

Even with a short book like *Dark Side*, many folks helped to bring this project to fruition. Many thanks to my editor, Kat Mototsune, and to fellow writers Robert Delaney, Terry Leeder, Kim Muzin, Sandra Rosier, and Maheen Zaidi. And special thanks to Joyce Wayne for encouraging me to consider attempting this project in the first place. Finally, I couldn't have written this book without support and patience from my family, SuYoun, Joo-won, Sawon, Martin, Ann, and my parents KJ and MS Choi.